T5-AFS-728

SPECIAL MESSAGE TO READERS

This book is published under the auspices of

THE ULVERSCROFT FOUNDATION

(registered charity No. 264873 UK)

Established in 1972 to provide funds for research, diagnosis and treatment of eye diseases. Examples of contributions made are: —

A new Children's Assessment Unit at Moorfield's Hospital, London.

•

Twin operating theatres at the Western Ophthalmic Hospital, London.

•

A Chair of Ophthalmology at the University of Leicester.

•

The establishment of a Royal Australian College of Ophthalmologists "Fellowship".

You can help further the work of the Foundation by making a donation or leaving a legacy. Every contribution, no matter how small, is received with gratitude. Please write for details to:

THE ULVERSCROFT FOUNDATION,
The Green, Bradgate Road, Anstey,
Leicester LE7 7FU, England.
Telephone: (0116) 236 4325

In Australia write to:
THE ULVERSCROFT FOUNDATION,
c/o The Royal Australian College of Ophthalmologists,
27, Commonwealth Street, Sydney,
N.S.W. 2010.

KILL CONWAY

Sheriff Gilpin reckons he knows the identity of the men responsible for a spate of arson and murder, but proving it is a different matter. He wires for help, and Deputy Marshal Stuart Conway gets the assignment. Conway finds a man dangling at the end of a rope. Then, he narrowly escapes a fatal dose of lead poisoning. His destiny seems to be Boot Hill, but Conway is a man of steel and much lead is going to fly!

Books by Bret Rey
in the Linford Western Library:

TROUBLE VALLEY
RUNAWAY
MARSHAL WITHOUT A BADGE
GUNSMOKE IN A COLORADO CANYON
TEXAS PILGRIM
THE DEVIL RODE PINTO
OUTLAW'S WOMAN

BRET REY

KILL CONWAY

Complete and Unabridged

LINFORD
Leicester

First published in Great Britain in 1996 by
Robert Hale Limited
London

First Linford Edition
published 1998
by arrangement with
Robert Hale Limited
London

British Library CIP Data

Rey, Bret
Kill Conway.—Large print ed.—
Linford western library
1. Western stories
2. Large type books
I. Title
823.9′14 [F]

ISBN 0-7089-5273-9

Published by
F. A. Thorpe (Publishing) Ltd.
Anstey, Leicestershire

Set by Words & Graphics Ltd.
Anstey, Leicestershire
Printed and bound in Great Britain by
T. J. International Ltd., Padstow, Cornwall

This book is printed on acid-free paper

1

DAY had already given way to night as Stuart Conway saw the dim outline of a body gently swinging from the tree in the chill wind which had sprung up in the last hour. He drew rein alongside and reached for his knife to cut the body down. It fell with a thud as the last threads of the rope parted. He got down from the saddle quickly. The cheek he touched was already growing cold and Conway decided the man had been dead for at least an hour. His hand brushed against something damp and sticky on the shirt of the corpse. Someone had either put him out of any lingering misery with a bullet or been intent on making doubly sure the victim would not see another dawn.

He estimated that Buzzards Creek was no more than three miles up ahead but there was no sign of the dead man's horse. Conway was reluctant to burden his ten year old dun with any additional weight, yet he had no appetite for leaving the corpse for the night scavengers. The body was not yet stiff and he elected to sit it in his saddle and ride behind, holding the dead man upright. They would make town within the hour.

A tinkling piano and less than musical voices emanated from one of the saloons, while lights peeped out onto the street from other buildings, but there were few men on the boardwalks and they took scant notice of the two riding one behind the other. The sheriff's office was in the centre of town, just off Main Street, behind the Gold Dust House, and it was in total darkness, the night shutters in place over the windows. From under the door a slim line of light glowed dimly, indicating that the place was not exactly deserted.

Conway lowered the corpse before

easing himself down, hitched the buckskin, and stepped up to the door. He rapped sharply and a voice called, "It ain't locked!"

He went inside. The man sitting behind the stained pinewood desk was resting his chin on one hand, partially hiding a lush growth of beard. In his right hand a pen was poised over a heavy ledger. Full lips sat slightly parted under the thick moustache. The eyes looked at Conway with curiosity. Conway spotted the star on the man's vest.

"Sheriff Gilpin?"

"The same. Who are you?"

"United States Deputy Federal Marshal Stuart Conway."

Gilpin smiled a welcome.

"There's a body outside," Conway told him. "Found him hanging from a tree three or four miles west of town."

"Who is he?"

"No idea. It was too dark out there to go through his pockets. Besides,

I figured you might feel that was your job."

"We'd best get him in here then an' find out."

"He's also been shot."

"Shot!"

A small silence developed as Conway gave him a moment to think about the significance of what he had been told. "Shot," Conway repeated.

"What's the point of shootin' a man an' then hangin' him?"

"Could have been the other way around."

The eyes looked thoughtful beneath a shock of hair that was parted in the middle and fell forward to cover his forehead completely. Conway figured the sheriff hadn't visited a barber for some considerable time.

"Suppose so," Gilpin conceded after a half dozen heartbeats.

Conway led the way outside.

As soon as they had gotten the dead man into the office Sheriff Gilpin said, "Nev Sawyer, homesteader. That's one less for Talbot to worry about."

"Talbot?"

"New empire builder in the territory. Has a big spread between here an' the border with New Mexico and aims to make it bigger. He's almost gotten the town surrounded by his property. Owns the Gold Dust House, saloon-cum-bordello, as well as the biggest general store in town to boot."

"And ruthless in his pursuit of riches, I take it?"

"You can say that again."

They laid him on the floor beneath one of the shuttered windows and Sheriff Gilpin went through the man's pockets. "Don't expect to find much," he said cynically.

He was right. The man's billfold was almost empty and his other pockets contained nothing but a red polka-dotted handkerchief, a stub of pencil and seventy cents.

"Not one of your wealthy men," Conway mused aloud.

Gilpin put the billfold and the

handkerchief in a desk drawer, then turned to Conway. "You mind stayin' here while I go get the mortician, Marshal?"

"Go ahead."

Conway looked down at the dead man with a measure of compassion, yet another victim of man's greed and inhumanity to his fellow men, according to what the sheriff had intimated. He would be interested to meet Talbot, the empire builder.

* * *

After Josh Wragby had departed with the corpse Conway said, "I could use a cup of coffee, Sheriff."

"Help yourself. I think there's still some in that pot on the stove."

Conway felt the hot liquid easing the dryness in his throat and warming his belly as it continued its downward journey.

"Let's talk, Sheriff."

Sheriff Gilpin gave him a rundown

on the men and women engaged in the art of survival, as well as the man who would dominate them all, by whatever means it might take, given the chance.

"He's an oily customer, that Talbot. A real gentleman when it suits him, but underneath it all a right bastard."

The last word in Gilpin's statement was spat out venomously.

"How come the residents around Buzzards Creek haven't ganged up on him, Sheriff?"

"The homesteaders tried that, but he picked 'em off one by one. Threats were enough for some, but the resistance of others began to crumble when Blair was found shot one night, right here in town. Three more families took it as a warnin' an' sold to Talbot soon after. Courtney Walsh was found on his spread with his neck broken. Folks said his horse must've thrown him, only his wife didn't believe it. She sold to Talbot at a knockdown price an' went back east."

The sheriff let out an exasperated sigh before going on. “Then the Osbourne house was torched one night while they were all asleep. They were lucky to get out alive. A few o’ the other homesteaders offered to help Osbourne build a new house but his wife was too hysterical to stay. Talbot gave them a few dollars for title to the land an’ they went back to Wisconsin.

“Another family had their horses an’ cattle die on ’em. Poisoned water, I reckon, but no evidence I could find as to who did it, except that they sold to Talbot. I wanna get that man, Conway, but I want to do it legally, an’ there’s nothin’ illegal about a man wantin’ to buy all the land he can get his hands on. That’s why I need help to gather evidence to nail Talbot.”

“How about the town folk?”

“Most of ’em are too scared. He’s gotten half o’ them over a barrel. Without his support they’d be finished.”

“You care to tell me how he managed to get a hold over them?”

"By loaning them money, then foreclosing before they could pay him back. Come daylight you'll see Ben Casey's general store, the biggest in town, an' folks think Ben still owns it, but in fact he's only the manager. It's an old story."

Gilpin took a deep breath, as if the tale he was about to relate pained him, then continued. "Ben was one o' the early settlers in Buzzards Creek an' he struggled in those first years. Not enough trade to keep a wife an' son when Roger Talbot showed up. Talbot saw an opportunity an' took full advantage. He gave Ben a loan for three months without collateral, but Casey must've been out of his mind to take it. There was never any chance he would come up with the money an' the interest in the time. Talbot then offered to buy him out but let him stay on as store manager. Ben had either to accept or quit town, with not enough money from the sale to start over some place else."

Conway could guess the rest. "Then the town grew with the coming of the railroad and the store prospered."

"And grew," the sheriff emphasized. "You should see the size of it now. You can buy everything at Ben's from a safety pin to a saddle."

"The only store in Buzzards Creek?"

"No. There is a smaller one that sells mostly foodstuffs, an' two others barely makin' enough to keep body an' soul together."

"Doesn't Casey sell kitchen goods for the women?"

"Some, but there's not enough profit in it for Talbot's liking. He don't seem to mind the competition."

"And there are others indebted to Talbot?"

"Bob Reid, the saddler, rents his place from Talbot. Talbot bought the place before Reid arrived. Bob would like to buy the property, only Talbot won't sell. George Taggart was on his uppers when Talbot helped him out with cash money, an' now George has to pay the rancher ten per cent of all his profits. Talbot has the same arrangement with Chet Handley, the lumber merchant. All nice an' legal, so I can't touch him."

"Quite an astute businessman, this Roger Talbot. Is there any man he doesn't own in Buzzards Creek? Apart from you, I mean," Conway added hastily.

"Doc Rickman, Eli Atkins, the lawyer, who incidentally takes care of all Talbot's legal work, an' the blacksmith, Frank Walmsley." Gilpin grinned. "He don't seem t'be able to get no hold on them."

Conway didn't need telling how Roger Talbot had gotten a hold over the lumber merchant. He might have loaned him money, or bought a ten per cent stake in the trade, with a little gentle persuasion. A man with a yard full of timber can't afford to make enemies. The threat of a little arson one night and the fear of losing a whole year's profit was almost as threatening as a gun held at the back of a man's head. Conway was already forming a dislike of Talbot.

"And you think Talbot is back of this murder tonight?"

"I'd bet my last dollar on it, Marshal. An' that reminds me, nobody knows I sent to the Marshal's Office for help, so . . . "

"You want me here incognito?" Conway finished for him.

"Can you work that way?"

"I noticed you didn't mention to Wragby what I was doing here." Conway smiled agreeably. "We'll do it your way."

"Thanks. If Talbot even suspected who you were an' why you're here, there'd be a bullet with my name on it."

"You sure there isn't one already?"

2

HE found satisfactory accommodation at Valerie Underwood's Rooming House, which would be cheaper and more homely than a bed in the imposing-looking Regal Hotel. Conway liked his comfort but he was not a man to squander his money needlessly.

Valerie Underwood had large round eyes and a closed-lip sort of smile, but Sheriff Gilpin had assured him that she was an excellent cook and took a special interest in the welfare of her guests. She inquired if he had partaken of supper.

"I had some trail grub around five o'clock."

"I could warm up a little stew for you, if you'd fancy that?"

Already feeling peckish, Conway accepted the offer.

After two cups of coffee he excused himself and returned to the sheriff's office.

"All fixed up then?" Gilpin queried, smiling.

"Odd little woman, but the homely kind."

"She'll look after you. Now let's go and see Mr Roger Talbot and acquaint him with your find. He'll deny all knowledge of the killin', but it'll give you the chance to assess the man for yourself."

The sheriff had earlier acquainted Conway with the fact that Talbot spent most of his nights in his suite at the Gold Dust Saloon. Apparently he was content to leave the running of the ranch to his foreman, Walt Martin, who knew more about cattle ranching than Talbot would ever take the trouble to learn. It seemed the man was a good judge of character and had the acumen to be able to delegate responsibilities to people he could trust.

The Gold Dust House was bigger

than most establishments of its kind, with a long mahogany bar stretching across one end of the downstairs room. The other end was furnished with the gambling tables; blackjack, faro, poker, and a roulette wheel, and the place was well lit. Roger Talbot was leaning against the bar, his gaze fastened on the sheriff and Conway as they approached him.

Conway's training enabled him to take in the man's physical aspects in a matter of seconds. He stood around five feet and nine inches, had a wealth of dark brown hair atop a smiling face from which brown eyes betrayed amusement and a keen interest in the two men ambling his way.

"To what do we owe the honour of two calls in one evening, Sheriff?"

"I'd like a word in private, Mr Talbot, if you don't mind?"

"By the look on your face, Sheriff, it must be something serious. Something to do with your friend here?"

His gaze switched to Conway,

scrutinizing the clean-cut, handsome look of him, the firm, dimpled jaw. Two pairs of brown eyes locked and Conway said, "I'm Stuart Conway, and yes, what the sheriff has to say to you is important."

There was a short hesitation before Talbot invited them to follow him to his office.

The stairs were almost as wide as some eastern hotels, with a mahogany, curving banister rail that matched the colour of the bar. As they went upwards a woman coming down favoured Conway with what she had cultivated as a seductive smile. He ignored her.

Talbot walked across the room and sat in a swivel chair behind his ornate mahogany desk. "Be seated, gentlemen."

They both ignored the invitation and declined the offer of a cigar as Talbot held out the box towards them.

The sheriff wasted no time. "Mr Conway brought in a body tonight."

Still waiting, Talbot asked, "Anyone I know?"

"Nev Sawyer."

"Sawyer!" Conway couldn't decide if the surprised response was genuine or not. "How did he die?"

"Lynched! An' then shot for good measure."

"Sounds like the waste of a good bullet. Who would do such a thing, do you imagine?"

"He told me a week ago that you'd made him a final offer, which he'd rejected."

Talbot leaned forward. "You're not suggesting I killed him because he wouldn't sell, are you?"

"I doubt if you would do it personally."

The Talbot charm vanished. "What's that supposed to mean?"

"It means I know of no one but you who could benefit from Sawyer's death."

Getting hurriedly to his feet, Talbot snarled, "I demand an apology for that remark, Sheriff, in front of the witness you've brought with you. Nev Sawyer was due to quit the territory tomorrow. My lawyer has his signature on a bill of sale signed this morning. I would have gained nothing by Sawyer's death."

"In that case, there's nothing more to be said. Just thought I'd acquaint you with the murder. My inquiries have to take in all possibilities. Good night . . . Mr Talbot."

The animosity between the two men was clear for Conway to see.

Gilpin led the way purposefully back to the street. When they were out on the boardwalk again Conway said, "I don't think you'll be getting his vote next election time, Sheriff."

Gilpin grinned. "I doubt if I got it last time, either. An' he's chairman o' the town council."

"That suggests the other members of the council — or most of them — did vote for you." Conway smiled back. "Or were you the only candidate for the job?"

"No. Talbot put up his own man, only he lacks charm."

The sheriff moved off to his left and Conway fell in alongside. "Where to now?"

"To meet Sean Murphy. His Stag's Head Saloon is Talbot's main opposition."

The two leisure palaces were no more than thirty yards apart and the sheriff paused before taking Conway inside. "To put you in the picture, Mr Conway, the difference between these places is that Sean allows no prostitution; Talbot thrives on it."

"Do I take it Sean Murphy is a friend of yours?"

"He is. He came from Ireland with his folks as a toddler, an' Ireland, I'm told, is a very religious country. If we go into Sean's private rooms you'll see a statue of the Madonna, an' that should tell you something about the man. Come on, I'll introduce you. He'll be very interested in Nev Sawyer's killin'."

* * *

Sean Murphy stood six feet tall, had unruly corn-coloured hair and eyebrows, and green, alert eyes. He weighed up the sheriff's companion quickly. "Glad to know you, Mr Conway. Welcome to the Stag's Head."

Conway had already looked around the main bar and games room. "Fine place you've gotten here, Mr Murphy."

"Nobody calls me mister. Just Sean."

"Then I'm just Conway."

"We bring sad tidings, Sean," Gilpin told him. "Nev Sawyer's dead. Conway found him hangin' about three miles west o' town."

"Oh, nooo." The 'no' was long drawn out. "Talbot?"

"No proof, but who else would you suspect?"

"He'll have the perfect alibi, but I'd gamble he was behind it. Be interesting to know how Paul Tessler spent the day."

Conway put in questioningly, "Paul Tessler?"

"Talbot's hard man," the sheriff

answered. "Employed as a bronc buster, but don't take orders from Walt Martin. Answers directly to Talbot."

Conway asked, "Do you really believe Neville Sawyer signed over his deeds to Talbot this morning?"

"Oh, I don't doubt that, but was Tessler's gun pressing on the back of his neck at the time?"

Unless the sheriff was way off beam it was not difficult for Conway to work out what had followed. Talbot could have taken legal transfer papers, drawn up in advance by his lawyer, Eli Atkins, gotten Sawyer to sign under duress, while hoping for some way to escape with his life, but once the deed was done, he could have helped Tessler to truss up the homesteader, then hastened into town and deposited the document with Atkins for safe keeping. Or quite likely there was at least one other man involved, and he or they, if there had been more than one, had kept Sawyer a prisoner until dusk, then taken him out and lynched him.

But it's all conjecture, Conway had to concede to himself.

"Has anyone else been lynched around here?" he queried.

The sheriff replied, "No, but Nev was more stubborn than the others who sold out to Talbot. He had more guts, too."

"You mean the others were scared off by what might have happened if they didn't?"

Like the ones you told me about earlier, Conway reminded himself.

"They all had families," Sean Murphy told him. "Sawyer had only himself to worry about. A man can be blackmailed into doing something he'd rather not do if his family are threatened."

Take my money and go or end up with nothing worth staying for, Conway interpreted. The threat of arson is a very powerful incentive for a man to take his family elsewhere when his home is built mainly of timber. Quantrell and his raiders had perfected the art of burning and pillaging during the

Civil War, Conway recalled hearing and reading, even though he had been only a boy during the conflict, too young to have been involved in any of the fighting.

"How do we find out what Tessler did today?" he asked them.

"I don't know about his day, but he was in here earlier, playing poker," Murphy told them, "and that's unusual."

"In what way unusual?"

"Talbot doesn't like his employees patronising the Stag's Head, and I can hardly blame him for that."

"Made himself conspicuous, did he?"

"Left in a filthy temper, bawling and shouting, less than an hour ago."

"What time did he arrive?" the sheriff asked.

"Early. The place was practically empty. He had a drink at the bar and got into the first card school of the evening."

"That would be about the time Sawyer was lynched."

Gilpin looked into Conway's eyes

and knew the man from the Marshal's Office was thinking along the same line as himself. Paul Tessler had been trying to establish an alibi for the time of the murder.

3

MUCH as Conway enjoyed his bed, sleep was the farthest subject from his mind as he came out of the Stag's Head Saloon alongside the county sheriff. He did not believe in wasting time on any investigation and the sooner he could gather more information about Paul Tessler the better he would feel. It would be easy for him to simply accept that the sheriff's suspicions were well founded, but as yet he had not met the man and he must therefore reserve judgement.

Roger Talbot had been affable enough when the two men first went into the Gold Dust House, and his anger in the office would be perfectly normal and justifiable in the case of an innocent man. Conway needed more time to make up his mind.

"What now, Conway?"

"That depends on what your plans are, Sheriff."

"I don't have any. It's the same old adobe wall I'm up against. Like I said afore, I've been runnin' around in circles an' gettin' no place, which was why I sent for you."

"In that case, I suggest you nose around a little on your own. Folks might talk more freely to me if you're not with me. Think I'll go play me a little poker in the Gold Dust House.

"When do we meet up again then?"

"I'll contact you. If I learn nothing of value tonight we could take a ride out to that ranch of Talbot's in the morning and ask a few questions about who was doing what today, especially around six or seven o'clock."

"In that case, I'll let you go on ahead. I'll come in later."

The place was buzzing but Talbot noticed his return and walked towards him. "Back so soon, Conway? How come?"

"I'm a gambling man, Mr Talbot. I was with the sheriff earlier because I'm naturally curious about why that man Sawyer was lynched and who did it, seeing I was the one who found him hanging, but that doesn't mean we think along the same lines. If you were telling the truth you had every right to get annoyed up in your office."

Talbot flashed his smile and became welcoming and agreeable again. "You play the roulette table?"

"Not me! I've seen too many rigged tables." He held up his hand as Talbot's eyes flashed angrily. "Not that I'm accusing you of such dealings, Mr Talbot. It's just that I avoid roulette wheels. Poker is my game."

Talbot shed his hard image coat quicker than a chameleon and was all smiles again in the blinking of an eye. "Then let's see who's ready to throw in his hand."

"Oh, don't put yourself out, Mr Talbot. I can wait around until there's a vacant chair."

"In that case . . . Ah! Let me introduce you to one of my men."

Conway followed the direction of Talbot's gaze and saw a man who was even taller than himself closing in on them.

"Paul!" Talbot beckoned with a wave of his hand. "I want you to meet Conway. He brought in the dead body of Neville Sawyer tonight. You knew Sawyer, didn't you?"

"Sure, boss."

"Conway, meet Paul Tessler. He looks after the horses on my ranch. Best bronc buster in the territory."

Neither man offered to shake hands, contenting themselves with an acknowledging nod. "Conway," Tessler said. "I heard about Nev just a few minutes ago. I can't figure who would want to lynch him."

If he's a liar then he's a good one, Conway decided. The eyes of the swarthy, unshaven, very dark-haired man never flickered as he spoke.

"What about the shooting?"

“What shooting?” as if butter wouldn’t melt in his mouth.

“Didn’t Mr Talbot tell you? Sawyer was shot after they hanged him.”

“Really? I wonder why, unless they shot him first an’ then strung him up?”

“Doubtful. He bled some, but not enough to support your guess. A heart that’s already stopped beating doesn’t pump out much blood, Mr Tessler.”

Tessler shrugged. “Whatever. Rotten shame though. He was aimin’ t’leave for California tomorrow, I believe.”

“Who told you that?”

“Why the boss told me.” He cast an innocent look at his employer. “Didn’t you tell Conway that Sawyer had sold out to you only this mornin’, boss?”

“I did. It’s a sad business, but let’s get on to more pleasant matters. Conway tells me he’s a poker player. Think you can fix him up with a game?”

“Not tonight, boss, if you don’t mind. My luck’s right out at the present. I'm headin' back to the ranch. It's been a long day an' I'm ready to hit the hay. Some other time, Conway, I'll be glad to sit with you."

With a shrug of acceptance Conway said, "I'll look forward to it. Goodnight, Tessler."

"Goodnight."

The two men watched Tessler walk to the door and go out into the night as Conway inquired, "Been with you long, has he?"

"Three years, almost. Very dependable."

And how dependable is he with that gun holstered on his right hip? Conway asked himself.

* * *

Sheriff Gilpin seemed to be acquainting several men in turn about the lynching of Neville Sawyer, questioning their whereabouts during the early evening, Conway guessed as he strolled from one table to another, watching the play for several minutes at each one.

When the lawman departed, Conway followed him at a discreet distance, careful not to give any watching eyes the impression they were together.

The sheriff strolled past the lawyer's office and the small store bearing the name of N. Sykes above the door, continuing towards the church at the end of Main Street. It was as he was passing one of the frame dwelling houses that a shot rang out and Conway dimly saw the lawman fall. Whether Gilpin had been hit or was simply foxing he could not tell.

Conway hugged the corner of the Sykes store, watching and waiting. He could no longer see the sheriff, an indication that Gilpin was still lying prone. Had he moved, Conway felt sure he would have seen him get to his feet. Ambushing a peace officer in the darkness was nothing new, but where was the man who'd fired?

Conway catfooted across the gap between the store and the first of the frame houses. He stood listening, but all he could hear were the faint sounds coming from the saloons. Edging forward cautiously along the front of the house, Colt .44 in his right hand, he halted again before sprinting across the gap to the next house. Now he could see the sheriff lying inert on the ground, no more than ten or twelve yards ahead.

He called softly. "Sheriff! If you're playing possum, it's me, Conway, behind you."

No response.

Conway moved up to the sheriff and knelt down beside him. He placed a finger under the sheriff's lower jaw, feeling for a pulse. The beat was faint but at least Conway's worst fears were alleviated. As he turned him on his back the sheriff's hat rolled off of his head and as Conway peered closer, he caught sight of a score mark along the felt that had not been there earlier. The hat was new, Conway had noticed and very clean.

His fingers sought for blood, but

all he found was a bump along the contours of the skull, about two inches above the left ear. The assassin must have been no mean shot to come so close to killing his intended victim, apparently preferring a head shot rather than the bigger chest target, but Conway guessed the sheriff was only stunned by the bullet that had creased his hat; the hat had probably cushioned the bullet sufficiently to save his life.

Faint sounds of running feet away to his left alerted him and he looked up quickly. Whoever it was had run behind the bank, the Rooming House, a small saloon, the big store and the hotel, but when Conway sprinted across the street there was no one there.

He rushed quickly back into Main Street, found it deserted, and accepted the would-be killer had made his escape. He went back towards the sheriff, then saw a shadow figure by the church; someone walking leisurely.

Conway ran on cat-soft feet towards

the church, only to find the man had disappeared by the time he got there. It seemed to be the wrong direction for the gunman, but he decided to check with the church minister. He knocked on the door of the house.

"Come in, young man. What can I do for you?"

"The sheriff has been shot, Reverend. Can I bring him in here? He's lying out there," Conway pointed, "unconscious."

"Let me get my coat. I'll give you a hand."

The preacher was only a few seconds and, as they hastened towards the sheriff, Conway asked him, "Were you taking a walk just now, Reverend?"

"Why no, I've been at my devotions. Why do you ask?"

"Then it must have been a prowler. I saw someone strolling by the church but he disappeared."

As they lifted Gilpin he moaned and began to stir. They carried him to the house and laid him on the couch in the preacher's living room.

Gilpin opened his eyes but it took him a few seconds to focus on the men looking down on him. "What happened?"

"Someone took a shot at you," Conway told him.

"I . . . I don't remember." His left hand lifted to the lump the bullet had raised. "My head hurts."

"Thank that new hat it's no worse. I reckon the bullet would have scrambled your brains without it."

He looked steadily at Conway. "You see who it was?"

"No, but somebody wanted you dead."

The preacher sighed regretfully and said, "A risk that goes with the job, I suppose. It's an evil world we live in, Sheriff."

A brief silence followed as the men eyed each other in turn.

"You've met Conway then," Gilpin said.

"Not formally, no." The tall, lean

preacher turned to Conway. "My name is Brunton, Mr Conway. I try to bring a little sanity into this crazy world."

"Glad to know you, Reverend."

"I think we should get the doc to take a look at our peace officer. He lives just next door. I'll go and get him if you'll watch over our sheriff."

"I'm alright," Gilpin protested, trying to sit upright and quickly falling back. "I don't need no doctor."

His eyes rolled as dizziness swept over him.

Brunton smiled and went out, returning a few minutes later with Doc Rickman, whom he introduced to Conway. The medic nodded in greeting, then concentrated immediately on the wounded man.

"Reckon you'll have a nasty headache come morning, Sheriff."

"Job's comforter," Gilpin muttered.

Rickman checked pulse and heart rate, examined Gilpin's eyes, then said, "Try sitting up."

"I already did. I didn't like it."

"Room start going around, did it?"
"Somethin' like that."
The doctor asked the preacher, "Can he stay here tonight? Best if we don't move him. He's concussed. Needs to stay quiet."
"Have to get back to my office," the sheriff protested lamely, making no attempt to move.
"Not tonight, Sheriff." Rickman was adamant. "Let your friend Conway do what needs to be done, then I'll examine you again in the morning. Whatever you have to do can wait."
"Bossy cuss, ain't you?"
"When I need to be, as you should well know by now." He picked up his bag. "I'll bid you goodnight, gentlemen."
The sheriff watched his departure and Conway turned back to the man who had impressed him as being both physically and mentally strong, yet now he looked like a big bushy baby, without the strength to stir himself. As Gilpin's eyelids shuttered again Conway turned

and made for the door, followed by the Rev'd Brunton.

"I'll take care of him, Mr Conway. You go and get a good night's rest. Are you staying at the hotel?"

"No. I've gotten a room with Mrs Underwood. Er . . . best have a bucket handy. Victims of concussion tend to vomit some."

"I'll do that. Thank you. Goodnight."

As he made his way towards the Rooming House Conway felt irritation crowding him. Not given to jumping to irrational conclusions, nevertheless he couldn't help wondering if the ghostly gunman had been Paul Tessler.

Would Roger Talbot actually order the killing of the sheriff simply for his attitude earlier that evening? It was hardly the response of a normal human being, but then according to Sheriff Gilpin, Talbot had a malicious streak in him, and the enmity between the two men was plain enough.

4

SHERIFF GILPIN was having breakfast with the preacher when Conway arrived, looking more like the man he had first met the previous evening. The lump on his head was plainly visible, but whatever pain the sheriff was suffering it did not stop him offering Conway a small attempt at a smile.

"How's the head?"

"Sore. Lucky for me you were around last night."

The preacher said, "Have a chair, Mr Conway. Coffee?"

Conway accepted the invitation to sit but declined the hot beverage. He'd had his fill before leaving Valerie Underwood's table.

"Dizziness gone?"

"Yep."

"Any vomiting?"

"Nope."

Relieved by that little snippet of information, Conway said somewhat dubiously, "You're fit to resume your duties then?"

Gilpin took his time before answering, using the minute or so to slowly drain his coffee mug. "I've been wondering if you'd care to take a deputy's badge?"

It was Conway's turn to hesitate as he chewed over in his mind the possible implications. Such an appointment would signal to all of Gilpin's enemies, whoever they might be, that Conway had taken sides. If the sheriff was on somebody's hit list it naturally followed that Conway's name would be added to that list. It would also imply that he was more than just an interested bystander.

"You think that's a good idea?"

"It would give you some authority around here. Mind you, I'd have to get permission from the town council. They might not look too kindly on payin' another salary."

That fact was some comfort to Conway. It would give him more time to assess the advantages as well as the debit side while the councillors considered the sheriff's request.

"There's a council meetin' tonight. I'm summoned to attend. I could put the idea forward then. Reckon I can count on the support of at least three o' the councillors."

Conway was reminded of something the sheriff had said the night before. "*If Talbot even suspected who you were an' why you're here, there'd be a bullet with my name on it.*"

Had he now changed his mind, or did Gilpin think that making him his deputy would divert any suspicion away from the fact that Conway had arrived in Buzzards Creek by arrangement?

The Rev'd Brunton pushed back his chair and got to his feet. "If you'll excuse me, gentlemen, I'll leave you to your discussion. Time I was about my business." He looked towards the door at the sound of knocking. "Ah! I think that will be the doctor."

* * *

Cleared by Doc Rickman to resume his duties on condition that he took things easy for the next forty-eight hours, Sheriff Gilpin wasted no time in planning his strategy. Their first call was on the banker, Solomon Johnson, a member of the town council. Gilpin introduced the two men and explained about Conway bringing in the dead man. He also told Johnson that he needed help to solve the mystery of who had murdered Neville Sawyer. Once he understood what Gilpin wanted, the banker promised his support at the meeting arranged for that night.

"So that's two of them on your side," Conway said. The medic had already agreed to support the additional expense on council funds to pay for a deputy. "Who's next?"

"Frank Walmsley, the blacksmith. He hates Talbot's guts an' we know Talbot will be against. He'll also have the casting vote if it should come to a tie, him bein' chairman o' the council. Talbot already pays more taxes than any o' the other citizens, him bein' the biggest property owner. It was the Doc who forced a tax on prostitution an' Frank supported him."

"And Talbot employs all the prostitutes?"

Gilpin grinned. "All those who do it openly in the Gold Dust, but I reckon there's one or two women in town who oblige the menfolk in secret."

"That's something you can't prove, I take it?"

"I've gotten enough problems without lookin' for that kind of evidence, just for the sake of collectin' a few more fines."

Walmsley was not the big strong man Conway had expected to meet, standing no more than five feet and eight inches. A wiry man with more strength in the slim arms than might be anticipated.

Gray eyes surveyed Conway candidly. Walmsley brushed a hand across his forehead to clear the grey hairs falling forward. The grey made him look older than he was. "Glad to know you, Conway."

After Gilpin explained what he wanted, Frank Walmsley said, "If the sheriff vouches for you, I'll support your application, Conway. I guess he'd find it hard to get himself a deputy from the men already here. Has to be a stranger to the town."

They left the blacksmith and headed for the lumber yard.

"Chet Handley might be a bit more difficult, what with Talbot havin' a kind o' hold on him. You remember I told you the chairman has a stake in the lumber yard?"

"I do recall. You think that makes any difference when it comes to council meetings?"

"No evidence of it, but . . . "

The sheriff shrugged the thought away.

Handley looked like the man Conway had anticipated meeting at the blacksmith's forge. A big, broad-shouldered man with black hair and a black bushy beard, untrimmed in the way that Sheriff Gilpin kept his facial hair under control. He paused in his sawing as Conway was introduced. A jovial man whose demeanour took on a more sober slant when the sheriff explained what he wanted.

"I was sorry to hear last night about Sawyer, but I can't see our chairman going for more expense, Gil."

"With your support and those I've already gotten, it'll make no difference how he feels about it."

"He don't like you, you know that. This idea'll set his back up again. You could end up crippled or even dead if you push him too hard."

"I nearly ended up dead last night. Somebody took a shot at me. That's what's makin' me dig my heels in now." He removed his hat to reveal the damaged skull. "Conway reckons this new felt cushioned the impact."

"I'd hate to have your death on my conscience, Gil."

"So you won't support my request in Council tonight?"

Handley was clearly reluctant to refuse, yet something held him back. Conway wondered what it could be.

"I need time to think about it, Gil But I promise you this, I'm in favour of anything that'll put a rope around the necks of the men who lynched Sawyer."

"Well that's a start anyway, Chet. See you tonight."

* * *

They collected their horses and rode out to the place where Conway had cut down the dead man. Neither of them expected to learn much. The rope still swayed in the wind from the branch that held it, and there were many hoof prints in the vicinity, most of them scuffed and many covered with fine dust from the trail, even though the hanging tree was several yards to the left.

"We'll try followin' the tracks," the sheriff decided, but then they discovered that they led back to the roadway, some heading towards town and others farther west.

"A deliberate ploy to stop you following their direction, Sheriff, but somewhere along the way they must have turned off. Let's ride west and see if we can find anything worth following."

Eventually, between two and three miles down the trail, they spotted sign leading north towards the distant mountains. They turned off over pastureland which the sheriff confided was now, with Sawyer's death, all a part of Talbot's range.

"We'll head for Sawyer's place an' see if there are any clues to be found there."

Conway doubted the validity of what they might find. There would have been no need to obliterate evidence of a struggle because that likelihood was not in doubt. What they needed were clues to the identity of the men who had abducted Neville Sawyer.

"At least they didn't torch the place."

The sheriff made the observation with some measure of comfort when they halted and gazed on the large shack that Neville Sawyer had called home. It wasn't much of a place, but adequate for a man living alone.

"Was he a misogynist, Sheriff?"

"Was he hell!" the sheriff shot back with scorn. "Liked a woman as much as any man, only he didn't believe in keepin' one of his own. Nev had only one use for women."

The knowledge did not endear Conway to the dead man. "Content to cook for himself, huh?"

"Good cook, too. I've shared several suppers with Nev."

Was Sheriff Gilpin also a misogynist? Conway asked himself. It would hardly be prudent to inquire, considering that at the age of thirty Conway himself was still unmmarried. In his case it was not a hatred of women but an inexplicable nervousness in the company of the female of the species.

He steered the conversation away from the subject of women. "Is it far from here to the Talbot ranch?"

"The house, you mean? About four miles. We'll ride over there after we've had ourselves a look around here."

All they discovered was what they had expected. The stove was cold and the ash pan was half filled with grey powder. There was no sign of blood or any indication that Sawyer had been tortured before signing over his homestead to Talbot. Horses in the pole corral had their heads over the top rail, watching them, as they emerged from the shack. Conway followed the sheriff as he walked towards them. They turned and shot away to the far side of the enclosure.

"Now that's funny," Gilpin mused. "Somebody's filled the water trough."

When Conway followed the sheriff's gaze he knew they were sharing the same thought. The trough, placed just on the outside of the corral, was almost full, and must have been replenished that very morning, maybe no more than an hour ago.

Who had done it?

And why?

"Somebody has an interest in the welfare o' these broncs, Conway, an' I don't need two guesses to identify that man."

5

WHEN they reached the ranch they found Paul Tessler being tossed unmercifully on a sorrel stallion, his shirt wet with sweat as he hung on grimly, pitting his determination against that of the horse. The stallion finally won the skirmish and as Tessler sat panting for breath he looked up at the sheriff, his expression revealing nothing.

"I thought you were in the habit o' cuttin' them afore you put a saddle on their backs, Tessler?"

Tessler climbed to his feet and slowly ambled across to the men still sitting their mounts. "Boss wants this one for breedin'."

"On your recommendation?"

"Naturally. What the hell does he know about horse flesh?"

"Makes a man wonder why he ever

took an interest in ranchin'."

"Ranches make money, if they're well managed. All Talbot is concerned with is the profits."

Conway said, "I get the impression you don't care much for your boss, Tessler."

"Then you'd be wrong. I'm no saint, Conway, but I take a pride in what I do, an' Talbot pays me good money."

Good money to one man was just wages to another, and the thought made Conway wonder about what else Tessler did besides breaking broncs? Only last night he had confessed that his luck at the poker table was on the wane, but it proved nothing. Tessler might be the sort of man who was content with little, only few habitual gamblers were so easily satisfied. It suggested that Talbot paid that 'good money' for other activities.

"Saw some broncs corralled over at Sawyer's place this mornin'," the sheriff said.

"Yeah?"

"Yep. Somebody had been an' filled the water trough."

"What's so odd about that? Those broncs belong to Talbot now an' I'm in charge o' horses."

"So it was you who rode over there?"

"It was." Tessler suddenly grew truculent. "Any objections?"

"No. I figured it was you." The sheriff looked around him. "Is Walt around?"

"In his office, as far as I know. Why?"

Gilpin ignored the question. "See you, Tessler."

The eyes of the bronc buster followed them as they steered their horses towards the ranch house. Conway felt Tessler's gaze burning a couple of holes in his back but he didn't look round. Could it have been Tessler who had shot at the sheriff the night before?

They hitched the horses and then the sheriff stepped up to the ranch house door and rapped vigorously. He opened the door and called out, "Sheriff Gilpin,

Walt. You in there?"

"Come on in. Office."

Conway closed the door quietly behind him and followed the sheriff. He was introduced to Walt Martin, the man who managed the ranch for Roger Talbot and acted as foreman over the men, except for Paul Tessler. Martin invited them to sit on rail-backed chairs and they lowered their butts.

"What brings you out here, Sheriff?"

"Tessler tell you what happened to Nev Sawyer?"

"He did. He's been over to see to the broncs on Sawyer's place this morning. Seems Talbot owns that spread now, too."

"Were you surprised?"

"A bit. I knew the boss had wanted to buy out Sawyer, but I'd gotten the impression the homesteader was being stubborn about it."

Conway was content to sit and let the county sheriff do the talking.

"He was. Seems like he had a sudden change o' mind, then he gets hisself lynched within hours o' puttin' his signature on the papers. Don't that strike you as funny?"

The warmth in Martin's greeting slowly evaporated as the dark eyes hardened. As Gilpin patiently waited for some response to his question, Conway sized up the ranch manager, estimating that his near-white hair had lost its original pigment prematurely, making him look older then he really was. The almost unlined face was that of a man not yet forty as he stared reflectively back at the sheriff.

"My job, Sheriff, is to look after this ranch, for which I am adequately paid. It is not for me to question Mr Talbot's methods of enlarging the property, so if you expect me to comment on what I think is going through your mind, then I'm afraid I must disappoint you."

"I'm conducting a murder inquiry, Walt. This ain't no social call. I'm lookin' for information."

"I know nothing about the lynching of Nev Sawyer."

"But you do know where all your men were between six and seven last night, don't you?"

"To the best of my knowledge they were all in or around the bunkhouse, after they'd finished supper."

"But not Tessler?"

"No, not Tessler, but then you know full well I don't count him as one of my men. He answers only to Mr Talbot."

"Where was Tessler yesterday mornin'?"

"I don't know."

"He wasn't here, on the ranch?"

"No. I didn't see him all day. He rode out shortly after breakfast."

"How about the other men?"

"They were all busy carrying out the instructions I'd given them."

"Can you be sure o' that?"

Martin countered with, "Can you prove they weren't?"

Gilpin's eyes stayed on Martin unflinchingly through a long pause. "I've allus had you figured as a straight 'un, Walt, but the man you work for is as guilty o' Sawyer's murder as the man who put the rope around his neck. I don't figure he struck the lucifer hisself, but the Osbourne place was torched under his instructions, whether you believe it or not. He's made threats an' intimidated folks until they've felt obliged to sell out to him an' move on, an' I mean t'get him." He stood up. "If'n somebody don't put a bullet through his heart first, that is. Be seein' you, Walt."

When Martin pushed back his chair and climbed to his feet Conway saw what a tall, powerfully impressive man he was. When he spoke Conway couldn't decide if the voice was triumphant or cynical.

"Won't you take a cup of coffee before you go, Sheriff? I was just about to take a break for a bite to eat. You're welcome to join me."

Gilpin took a few seconds to control his wrath, then said, "Now that's mighty civil o' you, Walt. My throat is kinda dry."

"You too, Mr Conway," Martin

invited with a friendly smile.

"I'm obliged, Mr Martin."

Martin led the way to the kitchen, where a coffee pot was steaming on the stove. Conway said, "There's one thing the sheriff didn't tell you, Mr Martin . . . "

Martin's eyebrows lifted slightly as he faced the deputy. "Oh?"

"Somebody tried to kill him last night."

* * *

The aroma inside the store was a curious mixture of kerosene, tobacco, boot leather, and new clothing piled high in an assortment of women's shawls, men's shirts in checks, plaid blankets, and pants made by Mr Levi Strauss, all suitable for hard wear. Conway selected a blue check shirt and wandered around the store, as if in search of something else. The man he assumed to be Ben Casey was busy serving another customer, while his female assistant patiently waited for a woman of middle years to make up her mind which of the half dozen hats she had tried on suited her best.

Hurricane lamps hung from the ceiling, awaiting new owners and the first touch of flame on wick. In one corner stood picks and shovels, making Conway wonder how far away the nearest silver mine was. On the walls hung virgin axes and large-toothed saws. What was it the sheriff had said? "*You can buy everything at Ben's from a safety pin to a saddle*." The saddles must be hidden some place behind the abundance of clothing, Conway mused.

"Yes, sir?" Casey said, mouth and eyes smiling, as Conway approached the counter. "One blue shirt? Anything else I can get for you?"

"Not right now."

Casey took the shirt from him and began to wrap it. "Lovely day. You must be new in Buzzards Creek?"

"And you must be Ben Casey."

"That's right, sir. How did you know?"

"Somebody mentioned you were one of the first traders to set up here. I guess the place must have been smaller in those days."

"Yes, sir, it surely was. Buzzards Creek was still in its birth throes in those days, and not much passing trade." He passed over Conway's change, then spread his hands. "Look at it now. The railroad came to town and the place flourished. I guess I just got lucky, huh?"

Conway leaned over the counter and said softly. "You'd be a lot luckier if anything happened to Roger Talbot though, wouldn't you?"

Fully aware that the legal niceties would probably mean that ownership of the store would not automatically return to Ben Casey, Conway chose not to mention it.

The smile vanished and the grey eyes looked sombre. Casey's voice dropped noticeably. "Are you trying to tell me something, mister?"

"I hear there's a plot to kill Talbot," Conway lied easily. "You wouldn't have any idea who might be behind it, would you?"

"Who are you? What authority do you have to ask me questions like that?"

"Right now I'm not wearing a badge: tomorrow I might be."

"Are you accusing me of being associated with a plan to murder our town mayor?"

"I'm not accusing you of anything, Mr Casey. Just fishing for information. I heard tell Talbot is behind the departure of all those homesteaders who sold out to him and moved on, too scared by the threats of what might happen to them if they stayed on to fight him. It seems there are those in town who don't like it. It figures you might be one of them."

"Do you really expect me to comment on a statement like that to a complete stranger? Who the hell are you?"

"Name's Conway." He picked up his parcel. "Be seeing you."

Casey watched him depart with mixed feelings, wondering if there really was a plot to get rid of Talbot, but reluctant to allow a glimmer of hopefulness to settle in his mind.

Somehow Conway got the impression that Ben Casey would keep their conversation to himself, but if he was wrong and he related it to Roger Talbot, then the would-be tycoon would surely have to reveal his hand in one way or another. If Sheriff Gilpin was right in his assessment of the man, the response might involve gunpowder and a dose of lead poisoning.

6

JOSH WRAGBY was busy making a coffin as Conway walked into his workshop. "Somebody else died?"

"No, but somebody will. I like to be prepared. Nev Sawyer's lynching caught me on the hop. Used the only two coffins I had a couple of days back."

It was no more than an hour since Conway had attended the burying of Neville Sawyer — just prior to planting the baited hook in Ben Casey's mind — and it was obvious that Wragby was not a man given to wasting his time.

Conway said, "Anybody in particular in mind?"

The carpenter-undertaker gave him a look that was not geared to give Conway the impression he thought very highly of his intelligence. A slight shrug of the shoulders was all the answer he got.

Conway decided to adopt a more direct approach. "I'm Stuart Conway, the man who . . . "

"I remember who you are." He stopped shaving the wood and fixed his gaze on Conway. "Now why don't you come right out with what you want to say?"

"You any idea who might've killed that man we buried a little while back?"

"If you mean do I know who put the rope around his neck, or who fired the bullet lodged in his chest, then no, I don't, but when it comes right down to who ordered the killing, half the folks in town need no more than one guess. How come the sheriff sent you to ask for my opinion? He could've asked me himself an hour back."

"Sheriff Gilpin didn't send me. I'm just curious, that's all."

"You mean 'cause you're the one who found him?"

"Right. I guess half the town suspect Talbot was back of the killing."

"Sheriff give you that idea, did he?"

Conway let the question hang in the air, then changed tack again. "This your own place, Mr Wragby?"

"Sure is. I'm not in debt to . . . ." He broke off suddenly, remembering his visitor was a stranger. In an attempt to cover his error he said with a smile of pride, "Built this place with my own two hands, with a little help in fixing the roof."

"Looks solid enough," Conway commented, looking around.

He was content to let Josh Wragby think he had forgotten his error as the carpenter talked freely about first coming to Buzzards Creek.

"I was raised in Pennsylvania. Learned my trade there. Fell out with my boss and decided to head out West. I knew there'd be work for carpenters in the territories that were opening up. Set up here on my own. Worked on most of the buildings here in Buzzards Creek, and on that ranch house that now belongs to Talbot."

"Plenty of work still?"

"Enough to keep body and soul together. I get the quiet times, but then there's others when I need to be in three places at the same time. Not like Sheriff Gilpin: he's gotten more on his plate than any one man can handle."

"In that case, how come the town council hasn't appointed him some assistance?"

Wragby's eyes narrowed. "You're a stranger here, or you'd know the answer to that."

Waiting for the carpenter to explain what he meant, Conway soon realized he was not going to get that information. The man was already using his planing tool, as if Conway was no longer there.

"Know anything about a plot to kill Roger Talbot, Mr Wragby?"

The hands ceased their movements and the eyes looked back at Conway again. "News to me, but if you go around talking like that, I reckon there'll soon be a plot to kill Conway."

"Sorta figured on that."

Wragby's eyes widened. "You mean you're deliberately hoping somebody'll tell Talbot you've been asking that question?"

"I hear he's a very careful man. Likes to keep all his dealings nice and legal so that Sheriff Gilpin can't get him into court to face a murder charge. The sheriff can only go so far, but I reckon it's time somebody prodded Talbot into doing something reckless, and you can pass that on if you've a mind."

"Oh, no! Not me! I aim to live to enjoy old age."

"Be seeing you, Mr Wragby."

* * *

Pondering his next move as he sat alone, finishing the apple pie Valerie Underwood had served him, the lady herself cut into his thoughts. “Was that to your liking, Mr Conway?”

“First class, ma’am, first class. I can see why you’ve gotten yourself such a fine reputation.”

She picked up his empty plate, that funny little closed lip smile on her face, eyes shining, and said, “Help yourself to coffee.”

When she had gone back to her kitchen he continued his musing, remembering the sheriff would be attending the council meeting very shortly. The two men had not met since the graveside funeral ceremony during the afternoon, so Gilpin was not cognizant of the bait Conway had been laying for Roger Talbot. Conway had his doubts about the effectiveness of his plan, thinking he might have to plant the idea in the mind of someone like Paul Tessler for it to prompt any action. It seemed unlikely that Talbot would hear of it prior to sitting down to chair the council meeting, but Conway would remain vigilant, just in case his guess was off beam. He decided to pay a call on Sean Murphy and get himself better acquainted with the Irish-born owner of the Stag's Head Saloon.

The body came hurtling through the entrance and across the boardwalk as Conway drew near, landing in an untidy heap in the dirt road. A man followed in more conventional fashion, but in one hell of a hurry. He hurled himself at the one scrambling to his feet, determined to finish the fight as quickly as possible. More men piled through the door from inside, keen to see how the fracas would end, followed by Murphy himself.

Conway recognized George Taggart from the livery stable, his mind registering surprise. George had seemed a friendly, peace loving type; not the sort to indulge in a public fist fight. How had he gotten himself into such a contest?

Sidling up alongside Murphy, Conway asked him if he knew what had caused the fight.

"The stranger said something George didn't like about one of my girls. George has a soft spot for Liza and this feller intimated she was nothing but a common whore."

Apparently George had jumped up and belted him with a right-hander. "I've never seen him raise a hand to anybody before," Murphy concluded.

"Who's the one in the red checked shirt?"

"Dunno. Don't recall hearing his name."

"Rode in this afternoon," another man supplied. "From Gallup, across the border, I think he said."

Conway's eyes shifted back to the antagonists. Blood was already pouring from the stranger's nose and mouth and George Taggart seemed in no mood to consider that enough. He continued to swing punch for punch, until the stranger hit the road again, flat on his back.

As Taggart moved in on his prone adversary, the man's hand flew to his holstered gun. Taggart was unarmed and with a swiftness that a mountain lion would have been hard pushed to better, Conway leapt forward, aiming a kick at the man's gun hand as the weapon was half out of its holster, fisting his own Colt at the same time.

The stranger let out a yell of pain as Conway barked, "Back off, Taggart! You've made your point."

Taggart flashed him a sharp look of rebellion, then slowly his taut features relaxed into a smile. He must have recognized that without Conway's intervention he could have got himself shot.

"I guess you're right at that."

Conway grabbed the stranger's gun and snapped at him, "Where's your horse?"

"At the livery."

"Well now let's you and me take a walk up there. On your feet."

The man responded slowly, his face a mass of blood. He looked a mess and Conway guessed he wouldn't be enjoying his food much for a day or two with his cut and swollen mouth.

"You'd best come too, Mr Taggart," Conway called to the livery man. "I don't want this hombre taking the wrong horse."

Outside the stables Conway suggested that Taggart bring the stranger some water to clean up his face. When Taggart returned with a bucket it looked as if, for a moment, he would throw the contents all over the stranger, but catching a glint of steel in Conway's eyes, he thought better of it and stood the bucket down.

The man took off his bandanna and dipped it into the water. He gently dabbed his swollen lips and nose.

"What's your name?" Conway snapped.

The man eyed him warily. "Jenkins."

"Well, Jenkins, collect your horse and clear out. We can do without your sort around here." He said to Taggart. "Bring his horse out, George."

As Jenkins mounted Conway said,

"The next time I see you I'll arrest you for disturbing the peace. You savvy?"

"If you're a peace officer, you should wear a badge."

Taggart stood beside the tall federal deputy marshal as the two men watched Jenkins slowly head back east, and he wondered if Conway *had* worn a badge before descending on Buzzards Creek with Nev Sawyer's body. "You act like a lawman, Conway. Who are you? What are you doing here?"

It was an opportunity too good to miss. "I heard tell there was a plot to kill Talbot."

"You mean you're here to protect him?"

The astonishment in Taggart's voice told Conway all he needed to know about how the livery man felt with regard to the percentage he was obliged to pay Talbot. If there really had been a plot to kill the owner of the Gold Dust House, then it was fairly certain Taggart would have been in on it.

"No, George, that's not what I mean,

but I reckon you'll not be paying him ten per cent for much longer."

"How did you know about that?"

Conway put on an expression of apology. "I'm sorry, George. I thought it was common knowledge. Now don't you think you'd best let Liza see you've come to no harm?"

The mention of the girl's name brought a different look to the man's face and, as Conway turned to walk back to the saloon, he smilingly followed.

7

"I GUESS I owe you, Conway," Taggart said as the two men neared the Stag's Head Saloon.

He was not quite as tall as Conway but his shoulders were broad and Conway wondered how Jenkins had stood up to him for so long. Those punches Taggart had thrown were really powerful.

"Good job I happened along. You were mad enough to kill that hombre." There was a touch of amusement in Conway's eyes as he made the observation.

Taggart laughed. "I sure was. Not often I lose my temper."

"You could've gotten yourself killed, too."

"I'll buy you a beer."

"Later, maybe. My belly's still full of supper and coffee."

Inside the saloon they separated, Conway making his way to the gaming tables, where his arrival prompted men who had watched the conclusion of the fight to make comments. One said, "I guess that Taggart owes you, mister. He was about to get a bullet afore you stepped in."

"I ain't never seen a man move as fast as you did out there."

"I reckon George'll be in your debt for the rest of his life."

Conway smiled in acknowledgement of the compliments, knowing that other men would buttonhole Taggart to tell him how lucky he was. As conversations lengthened Taggart would not be able to resist mentioning what Conway had said about a plot to kill Roger Talbot, especially to men he knew disliked the town mayor. The rumour would not take long to get to the Gold Dust House and then it would be interesting to see how Talbot reacted.

After a while one of the poker players decided to quit and Conway asked if he could take his place, now keen to establish himself in Buzzards Creek as a gambling man. He played well and at the end of the first hour he was in pocket to the tune of more than three hundred dollars, which made him less popular with some of the men around him. Having achieved his objective he did not want to antagonize anyone more than was absolutely necessary, and when he lost the next pot he took the opportunity to vacate his chair, much to the relief of at least two of the other players.

"I'll give you a chance to get back your losses tomorrow night, if you've a mind."

The council meeting was apparently more prolonged than usual and Conway began to wonder if it might be best to wait until morning to find out the result of Sheriff Gilpin's plea. It was hardly likely that Talbot would learn of the rumours he had been spreading soon enough to take action that night, but he decided to look in at the Gold

Dust before returning to the boarding house.

Sheriff Gilpin moved into the saloon only a few minutes after Conway had entered, spotted him and walked over. "It was a close thing, Conway, but I've been cleared to appoint you as from tomorrow. I'll swear you in then."

Still dubious about the wisdom of such a move, Conway agreed to go along with it, hoping the advantages would outweigh the problems it might bring him. He wondered if he should acquaint the sheriff of the rumour he had been spreading, but that could wait until morning too.

"Time I hit the hay, Sheriff. See you in the morning. Watch your back. Remember what happened last night."

"You think I'm likely to forget?"

They exchanged grins and Conway headed for the door. As he did so he was confronted by Roger Talbot.

"Sheriff Gilpin been telling you the news, Conway?"

"Only the bit that concerns me."

"So you'll be on his side from now on. I may as well tell you, he doesn't like me. If he could kill me and get away with it he would. How about you?"

"I'm no killer, Talbot, except when it comes to self defence. In fact rumour has it I'm here to keep *you* from getting killed. Seems like you've antagonized a lot of folks around here."

Now there was no need to wait for someone else to tell Talbot what he'd been saying, but Conway had no doubt confirmation would reach him before long.

"Expect you heard somebody took a shot at the sheriff last night, Mr Talbot?"

"I heard about it in council tonight. Doc Rickman used that fact to argue his case for a deputy."

"The gunman was no one who works for you then?"

Talbot's shoulders lifted and fell again. "How would I know? It could've been anybody with a grudge against

Gilpin. He's arrested a lot of men in his time."

A good cover, Conway knew, for any order Talbot might have given for the sheriff to be eliminated. The idea that Paul Tessler might be that man persisted. "*Talbot pays me good money*," Tessler had admitted that very morning. Bronc busters were easy to hire, but killers demanded a much higher price.

"Goodnight, Mr Talbot. Expect I'll see you tomorrow."

Talbot grinned confidently. "If you live that long."

Conway departed with a smile, wondering if Talbot had been joking or making a threat. There was no longer any doubt in both of their minds that from tomorrow morning they would be on the opposite sides of the fence: the fence that Roger Talbot himself had erected with his intimidatory methods for acquiring more and more property for himself, as well as a share in what he could not buy outright. Conway was now certain that the sheriff's hatred of the man was fully justified, convinced by the thinly disguised antagonism some of the other citizens of Buzzards Creek had shown towards Talbot.

* * *

Coming out of the well-lit Gold Dust House into the street made Conway scrinch his eyes in an effort to acclimatize his vision to the darkness. At first the night seemed like a blanket of pitch, but gradually, as he walked slowly towards the Rooming House, his perception of the buildings along Main Street improved. As he walked on some sixth sense told him he was being followed. He ducked in between the first two houses beyond the Sykes store and quickly catfooted around the back, heading towards the Gold Dust House again, Colt .44 fisted in readiness for whatever might be around the corner.

"Drop the gun, Mr Conway. I don't

miss from this range."

Reluctantly Conway obeyed the directive, wondering where he had heard that voice before.

"Now move back the way you came. I'll be right behind you. Head for the graveyard."

The Rev'd Brunton! Conway found it hard to believe in a preacher who carried a gun. Was it all bluff? Had he been suckered into surrendering his Colt pistol when there had really been no danger?

The graveyard! Was he being herded there for easy burial in a grave already dug? If Brunton did have a gun, with the intention of killing him, surely someone would hear the shot, but by the time they came running, Brunton would be back in his house again, and who would search the graveyard coming up to midnight? After the town dowsed all its lights the preacher could return and fill in the grave. It was a chilling thought.

Had the preacher been lying when

he had denied taking a walk the night before?

"Over to your right, Mr Conway. That's right."

Stepping carefully, Conway managed to avoid the mounded graves, his brain racing to find a way of escape.

"Now left and forward a few yards."

And there it was: a freshly dug grave.

"Before I kill you, tell me who you are and what you're doing in Buzzards Creek."

Conway turned round and faced his potential killer. Dimly he could see the gun in the preacher's hand, held as steady as a rock and pointing at his chest. "More to the point, Reverend, who are you?"

"You know who I am, Mr Conway."

"No, I don't. Preachers don't go round digging graves and killing people, so you must be something else."

"Let me assure you of one thing: Buzzards Creek never had a preacher who can preach the Gospel like me, but I suppose there's no harm in telling a man who's never likely to be able to talk about it what he wants to know, but I asked first, so quit stalling and tell me who you are."

"Tomorrow morning Sheriff Gilpin will appoint me his deputy. Until tonight I was just a gambling man, looking for new pastures, you might say."

"Did you win tonight?"

"As a matter of fact I did."

"Why Buzzards Creek? It's hardly a gambler's paradise."

"I was getting too well known in Flagstaff. I was on my way into New Mexico when I stumbled on that body hanging from a tree."

"I don't believe you, Mr Conway. I think you're a hired killer with a job to do here. That story you told last night about the sheriff being shot was just to cover up your failure. It was you who shot him but then you were afraid that man you said disappeared around the church had seen you, so you pretended it was someone else who'd shot the sheriff."

So the prowler had not been Brunton. Was it the man who had tried to kill the sheriff, or someone who had simply observed the incident and had not wanted to get involved?

"You're wrong, Mr Brunton."

Brunton continued as if Conway had not even spoken. "You've agreed to take a deputy's badge because it will give you the perfect opportunity to kill the sheriff and lay the blame on somebody else's doorstep, but I have a vested interest in seeing that nothing happens to Sheriff Gilpin, Mr Conway."

"You care to tell me what that interest is?"

"He's a good man, and he wants to see justice done. Roger Talbot is an evil man, and all who serve him deserve to die. An eye for an eye, the Good Book says, Mr Conway, Leviticus chapter twenty-four and verse twenty. And verse twenty-one says 'he that killeth a man, he shall be put to death', so . . . "

"And yet you would kill me, Mr Brunton?"

A short, harsh laugh came out of Brunton's mouth. "Only to prevent the killing of a man who does not deserve to die. I think the Lord would call it justifiable homicide."

In desperation Conway quoted back at him, "Vengeance is mine, saith the Lord."

"Think of me as His avenging hand, Mr Conway."

His finger began to squeeze the trigger and the gun belched flame and lead.

8

THE man was so eaten up with his own misguided idea of justice that he failed to hear the approach from the rear of a shadowy figure whose arm lifted and fell, clubbing the Rev'd Brunton to the ground in the instant he squeezed the trigger. Conway had thrown himself down in a sideways dive when he saw his rescuer's arm descending. The bullet sped harmlessly into the earth.

Conway climbed to his feet in time to see Sheriff Gilpin pick up Brunton's fallen gun and shuck out the remaining shells, then stick it in his pants belt.

"See if he's gotten my Colt on him, Sheriff. He suckered me into dropping it."

It was in one of Brunton's coat pockets and Gilpin handed it back to Conway.

"How come you were so handy, just when I needed you, Sheriff?"

"I saw you talkin' to Talbot. Figured it might be a wise move to follow you, the way you shadowed me last night. I guess this makes us even."

"You don't believe in paying your debts a moment sooner than you have to, I guess. Another five seconds and I'd have been a candidate for this new grave he worked so hard to dig."

In the darkness the sheriff grinned. "The exercise must've done him good. He's known as a man who likes a little diggin', an' it helps with council expenses. Sometimes saves us payin' a grave digger."

The sheriff had a sense of humour, Conway noted, in spite of the fact that someone had tried to murder him last night. Maybe he was heartened by the knowledge that the Rev'd Brunton was so anxious to keep him alive.

"What are we going to do with this preacher man, Sheriff?"

"Gimme a hand. We'll lock him up

’til we can get some sense out o’ him.”

At that precise moment Roger Talbot was standing behind his desk facing the man who was willing to do anything for money, getting an explanation for the failure to kill Sheriff Gilpin the night before. As their eyes held Talbot said, “Well now he’s gotten himself a deputy.”

“Not that Conway?” The voice was derisive.

“Yeah. That means double trouble. I want you to kill Conway. There’ll be another five hundred for you as soon as I see his corpse. Maybe then that dumb sheriff will get the idea it’s no longer healthy for him to stick around Buzzards Creek.”

“I’ll do it tomorrow. He’ll be back at that woman’s place by now, I guess.” He turned for the door. “Think I’ll have a session with Belinda before I head for my bed. She should make me sleep better.”

“Don’t forget to pay her,” Talbot

warned, dollar signs dancing on his brain.

* * *

Gilpin was bright eyed and welcoming when Conway arrived at the office. He reached into a desk drawer and pulled out a deputy's badge, tossing it over to Conway, who deftly caught it.

"Don't you want to swear me in?"

"Consider it done. I want Brunton to see that star on your vest when we talk to him."

"Is he good and mad at being locked up?"

"He's gotten a sore head, but right now he's eatin' the breakfast I took him. Might put him in a better frame o' mind."

Conway took the vacant chair near the door. "Talbot told me last night you'd kill him if you thought you could get away with it. I got the impression he was thinking you'd hired me to do it for him."

"Well now, in a way he's right. If he was the sort o' man who wore a holstered gun I'd be tempted to taunt him into usin' it, but he ain't, so somehow we've got to round up enough evidence to get him into that court room, in front of a judge, an' that means bein' able to put witnesses on the stand to testify against him. Right now I'd reckon there's nobody in this town willin' to take that chance."

"Be signing their own death warrant, you mean?"

"You got it. Let's go an' talk to the preacher."

Brunton was mopping the grease on his plate with the last piece of bread, his jaws masticating evenly. He noticed the badge on Conway's vest, then looked at the sheriff. "You've made a mistake with this man, Sheriff."

"I heard what you said last night, Reverend, but you're wrong. Mr Conway came to Buzzards Creek at my request."

Brunton looked from one to the other, unwilling to believe he had made a mistake. Eventually, after a long silence, he looked at Conway and said, "If that is true, then I owe you more than just an apology, Mr Conway. I was convinced you were here because Roger Talbot had sent for you."

"You made that pretty clear last night."

The sheriff said, "Seems t'me you've been foolin' this town for too long that you're an ordained minister, Mr Brunton."

"Oh, but I am, Sheriff. You can rest easy in your mind about that."

"Then how come you carry a gun?"

"For my own protection. Not even a preacher man is respected by the outlaw fraternity."

Conway said, "But last night it was to protect the sheriff. You were willing to kill me to make sure he lived."

Brunton spread his hands in a gesture of helplessness. "What can I say?" His head moved several inches to the left. "Are you going to charge me, Sheriff?"

"Well . . . you did fire that gun with the intention o' killin' Conway, an' it was pure luck you failed. Attempted murder is a crime in this Arizona Territory, Reverend."

"I know, I know."

Gilpin scratched the hairs under his chin. "You could help yourself by tellin' us what makes you hate Talbot so much."

Elbows resting on his knees, hands supporting his chin, Brunton didn't take long to decide to comply.

"I could hardly believe it when I arrived here and found Talbot in residence. Didn't take long for me to discover he was still the same evil creature, preying on other people's problems to make himself rich again."

"Again?" Gilpin queried.

"Yes, Sheriff. He once lost all his assets to a man he tried to outsmart. Roger Talbot has always manipulated the weak. He was like it as a boy. We were at school together in Illinois. He was a bully then and he's a bully now. I'm convinced he gave orders for the Osbourne house to be burned that night, while the family were asleep inside, but I don't have a shred of real evidence."

"You an' me both."

"I keep hoping he'll make a mistake and I'll be able to testify against him, and it's become an obsession. Maybe it's been burning inside me for so long it's warped my judgement. That's the only explanation I can offer you for last night, Mr Conway."

Thinking how close he had come to ending up in that grave, Conway found the preacher's explanation of no comfort. But now he was anxious to learn what had started this hatred. Surely it was more than mere schoolboy bullying.

"What did he do to you, Mr Brunton?"

"He killed my sister."

9

RECOGNIZING the question in the eyes of both the lawmen, Brunton accepted that he could not leave his bald statement as it was. An explanation of the circumstances was called for and without it, he could hardly expect to avoid facing a charge of attempted murder.

In his late teens Roger Talbot had played around with the girls. One of them had been the Rev'd Brunton's younger sister, who was only sixteen at the time, and she had become totally infatuated with Talbot, as young girls so often do when a good looking young man pays court to them. Swearing her undying love for him, Talbot had taken advantage of her youthful innocence and seduced her, and subsequent copulations between the pair of them had resulted in Nicole

Brunton becoming pregnant.

"She thought he would marry her, but instead he accused her of trying to trap him into marriage before he was ready for such responsibilities. We only found out after she drowned herself. She left a note for my parents telling them the whole story and saying how sorry she was for bringing such shame upon them."

Brunton raised his eyes to meet theirs again, but this time the question was in his.

Sheriff Gilpin said, "An' not a damn thing you could do about it, legally, that is."

"God forgive me, but I wanted to kill him."

"A natural enough response," Conway said sympathetically.

Gilpin's reaction was more blunt. "What stopped you?"

"I didn't know how. I was only twenty-one and I'd never held a gun in my hand."

"I'd have clubbed him to death one

dark night," Gilpin said grimly.

"With my bare hands I knew I didn't stand a chance against him. You'd be surprised, but Talbot is a very strong man. We were all afraid of him."

"We?"

"All of us who were at school with him."

"What about your father?" the sheriff queried. "What did he do about it?"

"Nothing. He was a very religious man, bound by those Ten Commandments. Thou shalt not kill," Brunton reminded the two men.

"But you would have killed Conway last night if I hadn't clubbed you to the ground."

"Yes, I would. I wanted you to find enough evidence of Talbot's involvement in the killings of that homesteader, Blair, and Courtney Walsh, to get him into court and convicted, I told you. I thought Mr Conway had been hired by Talbot to kill you, too."

The sheriff pushed out a short, harsh

laugh. "When you make a mistake, Reverend, you sure make a big 'un."

Brunton's silent gaze embraced them both, until he asked nervously, "Are you going to charge me?"

"I guess that's up to Mr Conway. If he prefers a charge against you I'll have to . . . "

Conway cut in. "No, no charge, Sheriff."

Brunton heaved a sigh of relief. "I ask for your forgiveness, Mr Conway."

"I guess it's time we let you go and get on with your work."

Conway wasn't quite sure what Brunton's work involved in Buzzards Creek, apart from officiating at gravesides.

They released him and he left shamefaced, still muttering his apologies to Conway.

"I wonder if he dare preach about forgiveness come Sunday?" the sheriff thought out loud.

* * *

It was decided that Conway should spend the morning acquainting the townsfolk of his new appointment and evaluate the reaction.

Store owner Norman Sykes made it abundantly clear that Roger Talbot's hold over the town was something he would like broken, only he couldn't come up with any suggestion on how it could be done.

"Jest plain greedy, that's what Talbot is," Sykes complained. "It's gettin' hard for decent folks to scrape a livin' around here. You'd think a man who owns a ranch, a saloon, an' half the property in town wouldn't want to be bothered with a store as well."

Pretending ignorance, Conway asked, "Which store would that be, Mr Sykes?"

"Casey's, o' course, the biggest in town. Ben Casey let's folks think he still owns it, only I know he was about to go bust afore Talbot stepped in. Talbot owns it now. Casey is just a paid dogsbody, an' believe me, he don't like that."

"Did he tell you that?"

"No, but I know it's so. I knowed him from the old days, back in Colorado. We wuz partners one time."

Maybe there had been a falling out between them, or it could simply be they'd both decided to go solo. But whatever the reason, Conway figured Sykes would know Casey's feelings as well as any man, so there was no need to dig any deeper.

As Conway left Sykes the man's resentment remained embedded in his mind.

Sean Murphy was less vociferous but just as strong in his condemnation of the mayor. He had offered to buy out Murphy, then when Talbot's bid had been rejected he tried again with the suggestion of a half interest. Again Murphy declined.

"He said if we were partners we wouldn't feel like we were competing for business," Murphy told Conway.

"He doesn't like competition. I don't like the way he does business. Let's face it, men will always need women, but I won't get into that side of entertainment. I pay my girls well and I won't stand for any of them getting too involved with the customers. Know what I mean?"

Conway knew what he meant, even though the word prostitution had not been mentioned. Having taken on the role of deputy he knew that keeping an eye on the activities in the saloons was part of the job, yet somehow he couldn't envisage finding the kind of evidence in them that would put Talbot behind bars.

Josh Wragby was quick to notice the badge on his vest when he called on the carpenter. "Nailed your colours to the mast, I see, as the nautical men say. Know what you're getting into?"

"Not exactly. You feel like telling me?"

"Sheriff Gilpin has made enemies: now they'll be your enemies as well."

"You care to name names?"

"Talbot for one. He opposed your appointment in council last night."

"Anybody else?"

"Be wary of Paul Tessler. He's Talbot's hard man."

The man who made the coffins seemed disinclined to expand on his observations, but Conway knew there was a hidden warning in his reticence.

"You mean he's good with a gun?"

"That's what I heard."

Conway left shortly afterwards.

At the lumber yard there was no need to introduce himself. Chetwyn Handley greeted him with, "Mornin', Deputy."

The lumber yard owner was sawing timber into boards, assisted by a red-haired, medium built man, whom Conway judged to be in his late thirties.

Handley introduced them. "This here's Harry Digweed. Don't reckon he'll be giving you any trouble."

"Howdy, Deputy," Digweed responded.

"Glad to know you, Harry."

It was Digweed who voiced what Conway guessed his employer was thinking. "Any trouble you're likely to get will come from the Gold Dust House."

"You reckon?"

"Sure do. Crafty as a wagon load o' monkeys, our mayor. You be careful there, Mister Deputy. Believe me, I know."

As the man's jaws clamped shut Conway also knew that Harry had said his last words on the direction from which trouble might be expected.

"Thanks for the warning, Harry."

The strength of animosity towards the mayor in the town was something Conway found puzzling. How had he ever managed to get himself elected mayor?

Sipping coffee with the sheriff a little later, Conway voiced the question. Gilpin admitted having supervised the poll himself and there had been no positive proof of any irregularity or obvious pressure on the voters.

"But that don't amount to a hill o' beans," the sheriff expounded. "Half the town had been warned not to vote for Ben Casey afore the election by Talbot's hired guns, only I couldn't get anybody to admit it. In my opinion Ben didn't want the responsibility anyway, an' only put himself forward as a candidate because Talbot told him to, just to make it look like a genuine challenge."

"You mean you can't prove that, either?"

"No, I can't. Matter o' fact, I'm beginnin' t'think the only way t'get rid o' Talbot is to put a bullet through his brain."

"As a federal officer, Sheriff, I couldn't condone such action."

Brusquely Gilpin responded, "You think I don't know that?"

Silence enveloped them, until the sheriff said, "Would you mind if I left you to do the rounds tonight? I've gotten some personal business to attend to. I'll be back around noon tomorrow."

It occurred immediately to Conway that 'personal business' could involve a woman, but he knew better than to pry. If the sheriff had somebody special he visited every now and then it was no business of anybody else. It proved the man was normal.

"Be glad to, Sheriff."

* * *

The afternoon and early evening passed quietly enough, with folks going about their usual daily business. Travellers came and went, some leaving the hotel and others taking over the rooms they vacated; drifters headed for the saloons and were easily recognized as such. So long as they caused no trouble there was no need for Conway to insist they move on.

The town was quiet as he did his last round, until an explosive sound arrested his walk as he neared the

Gold Dust House. All eyes turned his way as he burst in, Colt pistol in his right hand. The unfamiliar silence and the sight of Paul Tessler holstering his own gun, a body lying still on the floor just a few yards away and the air of expectancy Conway's sudden arrival had introduced to the scene set his pulse racing.

He stood for a couple of heartbeats, consciously calming himself, knowing instinctively what was expected of him. He walked over to the dead man, gazed down at the weather-beaten face, and knew he had never seen him before. The bloodstain on the man's brown twill shirt was still spreading around the heart region. Conway noted the twin holsters and the two guns lying beside the victim; knew without asking that this had been a trial of nerves and fast hands between the stranger and Tessler, but knew also that he had to ask the questions.

He took a step forward and looked directly into Tessler's defiant eyes.

"You killed him?"

"That's right . . . Deputy."

The 'Deputy' came out with a touch of contempt and a challenge that invited Conway to take whatever action he was prepared to risk.

Conway sensed a kind of hopefulness in the man's attitude that told him any attempt to arrest him would be met with a defiance which could end in gunplay. Without shifting his gaze he saw Roger Talbot standing at the foot of the stairs and a prickly sensation ran down his back. Was that what Talbot was hoping for? Did he want a shootout between the two men to get rid of Sheriff Gilpin's new assistant?

To Tessler he said, "Why?"

"He figured he could outgun me. Ain't no man alive can do that."

It was a direct invitation to dispute the claim and as men quickly shuffled out of the line of fire Conway was frighteningly aware that everyone in the saloon knew it.

"I wouldn't count on that," he

drawled with a well controlled casual air. "There's always somebody who can shoot faster and straighter."

"You looked at the body. I plugged him straight through the heart, and you can't shoot straighter than that. As for being fast, he never even got a shot at me."

Conway recalled Josh Wragby's warning and now he understood the extent of it. Tessler had orders to kill him.

"So you were better than him . . . if you gave him a fair chance, that is."

Tessler's eyes darkened. Conway had known his remark would anger Tessler, provoking him into action that seemed inevitable sooner or later. This challenge was not of Conway's seeking, but he knew he could not back down in front of all those watching eyes.

"It was a fair fight, Deputy. The other feller challenged Tessler."

The words hung in the air, a lifeline for the two men facing each other that neither wanted, both of them keyed up to settle the issue without further dalliance; both of them sensing the shooting match was only postponed.

Conway turned his head to the left to face the speaker. It was Harry Digweed. The tension slowly drained from the deputy's body and his steely gaze softened. He looked at the men surrounding Digweed and asked, "You fellers see it that way?"

"Sure did," one replied. "That feller was jest spoilin' for a fight."

"That's right," said another, with murmurings of agreement from others.

"Would you go and ask Doc Rickman to come over, Harry? Best to have the dead man properly certified before we bury him. Call in and ask Josh Wragby to bring his buckboard while you're at it."

He deliberately refrained from looking at Tessler again and turned his attention back to the dead man. Roger Talbot appeared at his side.

"You know this man, Mr Talbot?"

"No. He's a stranger to me. As far as I know he only hit town today. Drifter, I'd say, looking for every chance he can get to make a name for himself as a fast gun."

"You hear the conversation between him and Paul?"

"No. I was just coming down the stairs when the shooting started."

"Started?" Conway looked at him quizzically. "I only heard the one shot."

Hard eyes stared back. "Just a manner of speaking, Conway. Don't read more into it than I intended."

Conway let it ride. "Will you stand by while I go through his pockets? Might be something to tell us who he is."

"I doubt it. Men like him don't carry identification. But I'll be your witness, just so you can report back to Sheriff Gilpin that everything's been done nice and legally."

"Thanks." Conway tried to keep the irony out of his voice. He wasn't sure if he'd succeeded, but he was more certain than ever that the citizens of Buzzards Creek had good reason for disliking the mayor. It was only a gut feeling, but enough. The man was beginning to irk him.

There was nothing in his pockets to identify the dead man, not even a letter from a relative or a friend. Conway wrapped nearly three hundred dollars, a clasp knife, a pocket watch, tobacco makings and a comb in the man's own kerchief, ready for handing over to Sheriff Gilpin.

"At least he can pay for his own coffin," the mayor said dryly.

"Yeah. What about what's left over?"

"Goes into council funds. Helps to pay a deputy's salary," Talbot added with undisguised contempt.

A little less for the town's businessmen to contribute towards law and order, Conway surmised, wondering how many of the men who died violently in the area helped out that way.

Doc Rickman arrived and pronounced the stranger well and truly dead. Josh

Wragby removed the body, happy at the prospect of making use of the coffin he'd been working on that morning.

Conway wondered if the man was psychic.

10

SHERIFF GILPIN was back in his office by ten o'clock. He offered no explanation concerning where he had spent the night and Conway refrained from asking. He brought the sheriff up to date with what had happened in the Gold Dust House the night before.

"I got the impression Tessler was itching to draw on me. He seemed full of himself, confident he could kill me the way he'd gunned down that drifter. Did he ever make any attempt to brace you, Sheriff?"

"No, he never has. Mebbe he thinks killin' a deputy ain't quite as serious as a county sheriff, specially if he could do it in front o' witness who'd call it self-defence."

"M'mm." Conway eased out of the chair by the window. "If you don't mind, I think I'll take a ride out into the country and get in a little shooting practice."

"If it'll make you feel happier, you do that. How long will you be gone?"

"Couple of hours. No more."

Up in the hills, three miles north of Buzzards Creek, Conway opened a new box of .44 shells he'd bought from Norman Sykes. For twenty minutes he practised his fast draw and target shooting. He was satisfied with his speed but he missed his target more often than he hit it; not by enough to completely miss a man's body should the necessity arise, but by too much for his sense of pride. He would return to the same spot the next day and try again. Had Paul Tessler killed that drifting gunslinger with a lucky shot the night before? If the outcome had been brought about by prowess with a six-gun, as Tessler himself claimed, supported by the evidence of witnesses, then there might be an ability gap between the two men, which could mean an early grave for Conway. Already Conway had decided that a confrontation with Tessler was now inevitable; not a matter of if but when?

He thought of the woman he had met two years ago, Heidi Wilson, patiently waiting for his return, with dreams of a future with him. Marriage to Heidi held a lot of appeal, even though he was still reluctant to leave the federal service and embark on some other way of making a living, but he had vowed to return and he had no intention of allowing Roger Talbot and his hired gun to interfere with that promise.

Loping back to town he tried to unravel the tangle of slim evidence and pure surmise in the tactics that had been employed to persuade homesteaders to sell out to Talbot and leave the territory. Without any hard evidence and witnesses willing to go into court and swear to what they knew it was nothing more than guesswork, however accurate that might be. What was not in doubt was the fact that war had been declared between Mayor Talbot and Sheriff Gilpin, and now that war involved Conway.

And what of the hatred the Rev'd Brunton harboured towards the man he held responsible for his sister's suicide? How long would his patience for the sheriff to get the evidence he needed against Talbot last before he took his gun and tried to kill the mayor himself?

How would it all end?

* * *

Back in town he made his way to the lumber yard. Chetwyn Handley was in his office, which suited Conway. He wanted to talk to the red-headed Harry Digweed, and found him busy with a handsaw.

Conway dismounted. Digweed looked up and ceased his sawing, sleeving the sweat from his brow. "Howdy, Deputy."

"Harry."

"What can I do for you?"

"You can tell me the truth about what happened in the Gold Dust House last night."

The warmth of his greeting evaporated in Digweed's stony gaze. "What makes you think I didn't?"

"I can't help wondering if you were trying to do me a favour. Were you trying to prevent a showdown between me and Tessler?"

Digweed relaxed. "Mattcr of fact, Mister Conway, I was a mite scairt about that possibility. Tessler don't look like no gunfighter, but when he goes for that gun o' his he's faster than a strikin' cobra."

"But he's a bronc-buster, Harry."

"Don't mean a thing. The man loves horses an' I heard him say one time he loves the challenge in breakin' broncs, but believe me, Mister Conway, you ain't seen nothin' until you see him kill a man."

"You mean last night was not the

first time you've seen him in a shoot-out?"

"No, an' I don't reckon it'll be the last. Less'n you've gotten a death wish, I'd advise you to steer clear o' Paul Tessler."

"Thanks for the warning, Harry."

Digweed made Tessler seem like the fastest, most accurate man with a handgun the West had ever seen. Conway had survived a few confrontations with gunslingers himself, but, if Digweed's assessment was accurate, then Conway needed to hone his own skill to perfection.

Now why had Sheriff Gilpin not warned him about tangling with Tessler?

* * *

After supper he made his way to the Stag's Head Saloon in his capacity as a gambling man, but his reputation as a player of some skill had already spread through the card playing fraternity. No one was willing to give up his chair at the poker table.

He talked for some time to Sean Murphy, who gave him a potted history of the founding and growth of Buzzards Creek. Neither man made any mention of the gunfight in the Gold Dust House the night before and Conway wondered if Murphy was carefully avoiding the matter. He found it a temptation to ask Murphy what he knew about Paul Tessler, particularly in connection with his prowess as a gunman, but held himself in check.

"Well, everything seems quiet enough in here, Sean. Guess I'll move along and see what the opposition has to offer."

"Come in tomorrow night. I've got a singer coming in on the afternoon stage. I'm told she's worth hearing."

"I might just do that. Goodnight, Sean."

"Goodnight, Conway."

The atmosphere was much noisier in the Gold Dust House, where the girls were more interested in making extra money in ways Sean Murphy would not tolerate.

A well-endowed redhead was taking a corpulent man up the stairway, she with a seductive smile on her face and he with a silly grin of anticipation stretching his moustache.

Roger Talbot was standing alongside his barkeep behind the bar, surveying his domain. The smile he had been wearing disappeared at the sight of Conway coming in. The Deputy Federal Marshal had removed the deputy's badge from his vest and Talbot was quick to notice the fact.

When Conway reached the bar Talbot said, "You're not wearing your badge, Mister Deputy. Does that mean . . . ?"

"It means I'm not on duty right now, Mister Talbot. I was looking for that game Paul Tessler offered me the other night."

Talbot nodded towards the gaming tables. "You'll find him over there. New man in town fancies his chances.

Doubt if they'll let you disturb them right now. Stakes are getting a little high."

Conway ambled towards the table, intent on learning what he could by watching the tactics employed by the players. He got a shock he would rather not have experienced when he saw who the newcomer to Buzzards Creek was.

Talbot had trailed him to the table and Conway could hardly retreat without making his move look suspicious. He stood watching until the new man in town raised his head and looked straight into his eyes.

"Howdy, Conway. I've been lookin' for you."

11

ROGER TALBOT moved closer and spoke softly. "Now why would he have been looking for you, Conway?"

"He's an old friend," Conway lied.

Talbot was suspicious. "Friend?"

"That's what I said. Haven't seen Joe in four years or more."

"You'll have a lot of catching up to do then. Incidentally, I noticed earlier he's a two-gun man. That says gunfighter to me."

Conway's head turned sideways. "Take it from me, Mister Talbot, Joe can take care of himself."

"Joe who?"

"Blondell, but my guess is he won't be around for long. Joe is a travelling man."

"He's no mean poker player, either, it seems."

Conway looked back at the table, where Joe Blondell was hauling in a sizeable pot, and Paul Tessler was scowling. Tessler pushed back his chair and made his way to the bar.

"I reckon Paul might be touching you for an advance on his wages, Mister Talbot."

Talbot sighed heavily. "Some men never learn. He's wonderful with horses, but too reckless in his gambling. You'd best keep an eye on him, in your capacity as deputy sheriff. He looks fit to kill your Joe Blondell."

Now that would solve a problem or two, Conway mused, if Tessler braced Blondell. One of them would surely die, and if it happened to be Blondell, an enormous problem would be lifted from Conway's shoulders. He figured he'd best have a talk with the sheriff.

As he turned to leave he was halted in his tracks by the voice behind him. "Not runnin' out on me again, are you, Conway?"

He swivelled and fashioned a smile.

"Not this time, Joe. I'm deputy sheriff here now, so I've gotten obligations."

"How about your obligation to me? You still owe me five thousand, plus compensation for all the inconvenience you caused me four years back. I do hope you haven't spent all my money."

The smile slipped from Conway's face. Blondell said unhappily, "You haven't?"

"Can we talk about this tomorrow, Joe? Right now I need to find the sheriff."

"Unless you wanna belly full o' lead, we'll talk about it now. Outside!"

⋆ ⋆ ⋆

Roger Talbot leaned on the bar beside Paul Tessler, blissfully unaware of the small drama going on behind him. "Cleaned you out, did he, Paul?"

"Yeah. I thought I'd gotten him. Figured he was trying to bluff me."

"You figured wrongly." Talbot's

voice dropped to a whisper. "Looks as if your failure to get Conway to draw on you last night has worked in your favour. You'd have lost that, too."

"I'll get him tonight, boss. I need that five hundred now."

* * *

Sheriff Gilpin was just entering the Gold Dust House as Conway reached the door. It was the perfect rescue from his predicament knowing that Joe Blondell was not a habitual law-breaker.

"Sheriff!"

He turned to face Blondell. "I'd like you to meet an old friend of mine, Joe Blondell."

Reluctantly Blondell took the proffered hand of greeting the sheriff offered.

"Glad to make your acquaintance, Mister Blondell." The sheriff noticed the twin holsters housing pearl-handled revolvers and frowned. "I hope that fancy hardware is just for show?"

"I only use 'em in self defence, Sheriff. I'm sure Conway will vouch for that."

The sheriff looked questioningly at his deputy.

"Never known him get into a gunfight, Sheriff."

"I'm glad to hear it. We've gotten enough problems in this town without any new gunslingers fouling the atmosphere. Conway here had to see one o' them out o' town just the other night."

"I'll not be around for long, Sheriff, so you've no need to concern yourself about me. Me an' Conway were just headin' for my hotel room for a chat about old times."

"Well I hope that can wait 'til mornin', Mister Blondell. Right now I need to talk with my deputy."

Blondell covered his annoyance with well practised ease. His fear that Conway had gambled away ten thousand dollars, including Joe's share, was churning his guts with venom. "In that case, Sheriff, I bow to your authority. Just don't let him get himself killed afore mornin', will you?" He smiled with his mouth but there was no humour in the eyes. "I'd be right disappointed t'miss out on our chat after all this time, not knowin' where he'd gotten to these last four years, or if some gunny had shot him t'pieces."

"You'll find him in my office in the mornin'."

Blondell followed them out on to the boardwalk. The two lawmen looked at each other, with Conway wondering what had caused Gilpin to come looking for him.

"My office!" the sheriff snapped.

Conway looked at Blondell, gave a resigned shrug, and followed the sheriff.

With the door closed behind him, Conway turned to face Gilpin. "What's happened, Sheriff?"

"You tell me."

"What d'you mean?"

"That Blondell is no friend of yours now, is he?"

Surprised by the sheriff's perception, Conway asked, "How did you know that?"

"He wasn't smilin' an he had both hands on his gunbutts when I walked into the saloon, so what's goin' on?"

Conway took the chair by the window and pushed his hat back from his brow. "It's a long story, Sheriff."

"I ain't sleepy, so let's hear it."

For half a dozen heart-beats Conway composed himself, wondering just how much to impart to his inquisitor, then he began to explain his predicament concerning Joe Blondell.

"Four years back I was sent out to recover ten thousand dollars that had been stolen from a train nearly six years earlier. Most of the soldiers escorting that money were murdered by bandits, aided by two of the escort detail."

The sheriff cut in. "I seem to recall readin' about that. The train robbery an' all that killin', I mean."

"Only one of those soldiers lived to tell the tale, and he was subsequently sent to Yuma Prison for five years on a charge of raping a Mexican woman, but there was some doubt as to whether he was guilty of that or not.

"We knew," Conway went on, "when Nate Quincey was due for release from Yuma and that he was the only man alive who knew where that money had been cached.

"It was my job to track him from the prison, but we also knew that other people were very much aware of what was likely to happen. Like now, I was posing as a professional gambler down in Yuma well before Quincey's release date, and ironically I was approached by a man named McKurdy who asked me to help him lift that money . . ."

"Not knowing you were a federal agent," Gilpin assumed aloud.

"Exactly. I played along with his plan, partly because there was no way I could refuse and still go after Quincey, and in part because I knew I might need help against other parties intent on relieving Quincey of his nest egg. As it happened, McKurdy got himself killed, but to spare you the gory details of all the other killings, the money — in two metal boxes — had been unearthed, and there was only me and Joe Blondell left. I had the money, but Joe had me trapped. We did a deal I had no intention of honouring."

The sheriff leaned back in his chair. "I can guess the rest. You agreed to take five thousand apiece, then you somehow managed to overpower Blondell and escaped with the whole ten thousand, leavin' him with nothin'."

Conway nodded. "Uhuh. My problem is, Sheriff, that if I now tell him I was working for the government I'll have to show my hand here in Buzzards Creek."

"And he might not believe you. In his boots I'd be tempted t'think you were makin' excuses for cheatin' on me."

"So what do I do about it, Sheriff?"

The sheriff snorted. "Hell, Conway! This is another dilemma we could well do without. Whether he believes you or not, he'll be so mad he'll kill you!"

"He might try, but even if he didn't, he's more than likely to let it slip I'm still employed by the Federal Office."

Gilpin considered that possibility and didn't like it, but he immediately found a way out of the problem. "Would that be such a bad thing? I could let it be known you'd wormed your way into my confidence and tricked me into takin' you on as my deputy."

"All out in the open, you mean? Me against Talbot, here to investigate what's been going on around here?"

"Best if we sleep on it, but right now it seems the only way out o' this dilemma Joe Blondell has brought with him."

Killing a deputy federal marshal was a prospect few men would consider, because everyone knew that when a government agent was killed they sent another one to track down the killer.

Federal men were relentless in the pursuit of any man who murdered one of their own and no man in his right mind would risk a rope around his neck. Conway's fear was that Joe Blondell might not believe he had handed over all that loot to the federal marshal. He wanted five thousand dollars from Conway, plus interest, and there was no way he was going to get it.

12

"I'LL walk you back to Valerie Underwood's place. No sense in you takin' unnecessary risks."

"No need, Sheriff. Joe is not going to gun me down as long as he thinks there's the slightest hope of him getting money out of me."

"You think not?" Gilpin scratched his beard. "Yeah, I suppose you're right. Best if you get here early in the mornin' though; make him come here t'see you."

Getting to his feet and pulling his hat forward again, Conway agreed that was a good idea and went out into the night. For several minutes he stood behind the Gold Dust House, peering into the darkness, accustoming his eyes to the change from artificial light, and listening for sounds of movement.

Two men came out of the saloon and

headed off to their beds, but Conway knew that activity in the Gold Dust would carry on for some time yet. It was still early for some men.

He moved into Main Street and turned right, past the lawyer's office and the Sykes store. As he crossed the road to go to the Rooming House somebody took a shot at him. He was never quite sure if he heard the shot first or felt the slug rip through his left arm. He grabbed for his gun in a reflex action, despite the shock of being hit, and threw himself to the ground, half way across the street, an easy target for the man to shoot at again.

Rolling fast he saw the flame as another shot sped his way and thanked his lucky stars it missed. He fired at the shadowy figure thirty yards away and fancied he heard the gunman gasp.

The shadow moved and melted into the night. Conway jumped to his feet and gave chase but he was too late. Wherever the man had gone his escape must have been well planned. Conway stood in the side street leading up to the sheriff's office and waited, wondering if his would-be killer had gone into the Gold Dust House. If he had been hit it seemed unlikely. A wounded man invites questions he may not wish to answer.

Men came out of the saloon to investigate the shooting and Conway barked, "You see anybody go in there just now?"

They answered in the negative, and then Conway found the sheriff at his side.

"What was all the shootin' about?"

"Somebody tried to kill me."

"So you were wrong. Blondell believes you've welched on him."

"No, Sheriff, I don't believe it was Joe."

Joe Blondell himself appeared and asked, "Did I hear somebody takin' my name in vain?"

"Were you on the street a couple minutes ago, Blondell?"

"No, Sheriff, I wasn't. There must be a dozen witnesses who could tell you I was inside the saloon all the time. Went back inside after you left with Conway an' never came out again. What happened?"

Conway told him. As he did so he was vaguely aware of the diminishing sound of hoofbeats.

"You hit?"

"Left arm. I'd best get along and see Doc Rickman."

"You want I should come along?" Blondell offered.

The sheriff quickly put that idea out of his mind. "I'll take him, Blondell. You get back to whatever it was you were doin'. All o' you, get back inside."

There was no doubt in Conway's mind that the shot had been aimed with murderous intent. Somebody wanted him out of the way and he needed only one guess as to the identity of that man. Roger Talbot was probably not the one behind the gun, but it was a safe bet he had ordered the assassin's attempt. As Doc Rickman cleaned up the wound Conway recalled the sound of that horse leaving town while he was telling Joe Blondell about the gunman. If all he'd been told was correct, then it was some small comfort to know that Paul Tessler might be fast and accurate at close range, but at a distance his aim was faulty.

* * *

Despite the laudanum Doc Rickman had given him to help deaden the pain, Conway spent a restless night. The bullet had torn a deep gash through the muscle of his upper arm, missing the bone by a fraction of an inch, and as the effects of the drug wore off the throbbing became continuous, accompanied by an intense soreness. When he could no longer find any way to lie comfortably he got up, washed himself, and dressed. He was downstairs by the time Valerie

Underwood began raking out the ashes at the bottom of the stove.

"You're up early, Mr Conway."

"Couldn't sleep. Don't mind me, I'm in no hurry for breakfast."

"I'll get you some coffee as soon as it's hot."

Through the hours of tossing and turning he had made up his mind to pay Paul Tessler a visit out at the ranch. He might not be there, but Conway figured that was his escape hole, the place he used not only as a base for his working day, but where he found time to relax and calm down after his better paid activities. Conway was eager to see if Tessler was nursing a wound. If he was, then how bad was it?

He recognized he could be mistaken, but a wounded Tessler would be all the confirmation he needed that it was the bronc-buster who had tried to kill him the night before.

* * *

As agreed with Sheriff Gilpin, he arrived early at the law office, aware that when Joe Blondell had himself a comfortable bed he was reluctant to leave it. Conway recalled that early morning was not Blondell's best time of day; he was often morose and silent until around mid-morning. There was always the chance that his eagerness to get to grips with Conway concerning the loot he felt he'd been cheated out of might get him abroad earlier than usual, and Conway was still unsure how he was going to pacify the gambler. Lady Luck had obviously been smiling on Joe recently, judging by the stakes he had been playing for the previous evening, but a man deprived of five thousand dollars he had felt was his can be a real angry hombre, especially when he has been searching for the man who robbed him for four years.

"How's the arm?"

"Sore, Sheriff."

Conway sank into the chair by the window, hoping Gilpin would have some solution to his problem.

"You come up with any fresh ideas, Sheriff?"

Gilpin scratched his bearded chin. "I did wonder if it might be a good idea for me to tell Blondell that money the two o' you recovered belonged to the Army."

"He already knew that at the time he went after it with his pard."

"Can't do any harm t'remind him an' it'll sound better comin' from me."

Conway pondered the suggestion, yet knowing that Blondell's mind would be locked against anything that ran contrary to already set ambitions.

"Four years is a long time for a man to harbour a grudge, Sheriff, eating away inside him like the lung disease. Five thousand dollars is a lot of money, even to Joe Blondell, and I can't blame him for thinking he was robbed."

Sheriff Gilpin agreed. "That's a fact. Ain't no denyin' it, but we have t'do what we can t'get the anger out o' him. We've gotten enough problems without

Blondell pilin' up more."

"Well, I guess it might sound more genuine, coming from you."

* * *

Blondell listened in silence, a smile on his face that said '*Pull the other one*.' When the sheriff had finished his explanation Blondell said, "You really believe that, Sheriff?"

"You can't deny facts, Blondell. Conway handed over the whole ten thousand to the federal marshal."

"The only facts you've gotten are what this lyin', cheatin', robbin', sonofabitch has told you!" He looked across to Conway. "I want my five thousand, Conway, with interest. We had a deal."

"I had to make that deal, Joe, otherwise you'd have killed me and the federal marshal would have sent somebody else to recover that money."

The sheriff said, "If Conway was the rogue you make him out to be, how come he didn't kill you, Blondell? Accordin' to what he told me, he surely had the chance."

It was an observation that silenced the gambler. He could not deny, even to himself, that at some stage back in that ghost town Conway could have gotten the drop on him and, if all the hatred he had harboured against the man were justified, then such a man would not have spared his life.

"You ever know me cheat at poker, Joe?"

There was a long silence as the men eyed each other, Blondell reluctant to accept that Conway had been despatched to recover the stolen money on behalf of the U.S. Government, while Conway and Gilpin waited impatiently to see if they had convinced him that the money could never have been his.

"Five thousand is a lot o' money, Conway!"

"I know, Joe, but you knew as well as I did that it was stolen money. Neither of us had any rightful claim to it."

Again the sheriff put in his pennyworth. "Conway tells me you're not the kind o' man who goes around robbin' folks, Blondell, so why can't you see it would've been wrong for you t'take that five thousand?"

"The Government is fair game, ain't it?"

The sheriff's answer was quiet but firm. "No, it ain't."

Perhaps it was Sheriff Gilpin's reasoned arguing that finally persuaded Joe Blondell that he should look to his conscience.

"Hell, Conway! I could kill you!"

"But you won't, will you, Joe?"

Blondell got to his feet, pointed his forefinger and snarled, "Don't count on it! I shoulda killed you four years back when I had the chance. I coulda put a bullet in you an' taken the whole ten thousand for myself. Remember, Conway, you're damned lucky to be alive, an' just stay out o' my way in future."

As he turned to leave the sheriff called him back.

"What is it now?"

"I'd be obliged if you'd keep what we've told you to yourself. Conway is here in Buzzards Creek on federal business. We'd prefer that not to be known around here till his investigation is completed."

Blondell turned on his heels and went out without another word, making no attempt to conceal his fury as he slammed the door shut behind him.

"You think he'll keep his mouth shut, Conway?"

"I think so, but I guess I owe you, Sheriff. I'd never have been able to convince him on my own."

"I didn't do it for you. I did it for me."

Conway knew the county sheriff made his proclamation with tongue in cheek. "If it's all the same to you, Sheriff, I'd like to ride out and see if Paul Tessler is nursing a wound of any sort?"

"Ain't that a bit like stickin' your head into a lion's mouth?"

"Only if he's a wounded lion. If he isn't, then I'll have to rethink my suspicions."

13

THE grass had grown from green to gold under the blaze of sun day after day. Conway drew rein, removed his hat and wiped the stained, damp sweatband with his kerchief. Setting out on this mission to confront Paul Tessler had not eased the throbbing in his arm, but at least his gun hand was free to work if the need should arise. He had toyed briefly with the idea of asking Doc Rickman to give him another dose of laudanum to ease the pain after he had dressed the wound, but quickly rejected it. If he did need to pull his gun on Tessler he did not want his mind or his reflexes dulled by the morphine mixture.

When he reached the ranch he headed straight for the corral, not really expecting Tessler to be at work there. The whole place was silent until footsteps came from the house. It was Walt Martin. His mouth fashioned a half smile but there was suspicion in his eyes.

"Conway. What brings you back so soon?"

"I was hoping for a word or two with Tessler."

"I haven't seen him today. You might try the bunkhouse."

"Thanks."

Conway dismounted and hitched the dun, then walked slowly towards the bunkhouse. As he drew nearer he catfooted towards the open doorway, halted, and listened intently. He turned at the sound of footfalls and saw Martin had followed him, that look of suspicion even more evident. Conway knew instantly that it was his cautious approach to the bunkhouse that had alerted the ranch manager to something not quite right.

"What are you up to, Conway? Why don't you call out or go inside and look for Paul?"

Brain ice cool, Conway said quietly, "I believe he was shot last night, in which case he'll be jumpy. I don't want to invite a bullet."

Martin's gaze was scornful. He called out, "Are you in there, Paul?"

There was no answer. Martin hurried inside, Conway close behind him. They found Tessler lying on his bunk, eyes shuttered, the look of death on his face.

Martin shook him but the eyes remained closed. He felt for a pulse and couldn't find one. Then he noticed the profusion of blood, red and sticky all around Tessler's waistline. He turned to face Conway. "You were right. I think he's dead."

The questioning look Martin fastened on Conway called for an answer.

Conway told him, "He tried to kill me last night. I thought I might have hit him with my return fire, but I wasn't sure."

"Why would he try to kill you, Conway?"

Conway moved forward and gripped

Tessler's left wrist, feeling for any sign of life as he replied, "Because Talbot instructed him to do just that."

"I don't believe you."

With a shrug Conway said, releasing Tessler's wrist, "There's the evidence, right in front of you. I wonder why none of your hands noticed he'd been shot this morning?"

"Paul is a loner. He doesn't fraternize with the men who ride range. Even eats after everybody else has finished."

"Did."

"What?"

"He did eat after the others. He's dead, Mister Martin. Sorry I can't give you a hand with him, but he ruined one of my arms last night. I can't help you lift him."

In an effort to convince Martin that what he was telling him was the truth, Conway unbuttoned his left sleeve and pulled it high to reveal the bandaged wound on his arm. Martin looked at it in silence, seemingly at least partially convinced.

"I told you a few minutes ago I suspected he'd been shot last night. Now you know why."

He went back outside and headed for his horse, reflecting that dead men don't talk. This whole business was far too frustrating for any man. No wonder Sheriff Gilpin had asked for help.

* * *

"Damnation!" the sheriff exploded. "What happened last night makes me more sure than ever that I'm right about Talbot, but we can't arrest him on suspicion. Pity Tessler didn't live long enough to talk."

"That's what I've been thinking."

Gilpin eyed Conway speculatively. "But Talbot don't know he didn't. What say we bluff him into thinkin' Tessler confirmed what we suspect?"

"Still only circumstantial evidence, Sheriff. We'd have a hard time convincing a jury. Eli Atkins would probably defend him and he'll know the testimony of a dead man carries no weight in a court of law."

The sheriff's shoulders sagged. Conway was reluctant to tell him that a trial — even if it was only a show trial — would convince Talbot's enemies of his guilt, and some of them might take the law into their own hands. As a Federal officer he would be duty bound to oppose any such action. The law was intended to protect a suspect until he was proven guilty. There had already been too much vigilante justice meted out, with many innocent men left dangling at the end of a rope. The fact that Conway himself had discovered Neville Sawyer in that final predicament grated in his guts, yet he believed in the due processes of the law and wanted whoever had been responsible convicted legally.

If Paul Tessler had lived through the night and Conway had been able to arrest him, which he doubted, given the man's appetite for killing and the likelihood that he had been at least involved in the murder of Sawyer, the wrangler would never have given evidence against his boss.

After a couple of minutes silent contemplation the sheriff said, "Maybe you should pay Talbot a visit, seein' as you're the one who found Tessler dead. Look kinda funny if you don't."

"I guess you're right about that."

* * *

There was no sign of Talbot in the saloon, but Joe Blondell sat at a corner table playing solo. Conway ignored him and walked up to the barkeep, who told him that Talbot was in his office. Blondell watched Conway climb the stairs, then disappear from view, his fury mounting again as he recalled lost opportunities.

Talbot called "Come in!" when Conway knocked on his office door. "Howdy, Conway. How's the arm?"

"Sore, but at least I know who shot me."

A wary look crept into Talbot's eyes. "Who?"

"Paul Tessler."

Talbot forced out a strangulated laugh. "You're crazy. Why would Paul want to shoot you?"

"We both know the answer to that."

"Just what are you implying, Conway?"

"He tried to kill me under your orders, but you'll have to look around for another gunny. Tessler died this morning."

The expression on Talbot's face set in disbelief. For several heartbeats he stared at Conway, then tried to shrug away what he had been told as some kind of ruse. "You're having me on!"

"No. I expect Walt Martin will confirm the facts before nightfall."

"How did he die?"

"Lead poisoning, or if you prefer it, loss of blood. You see when I fired back at him last night my shot did more harm to him than his did to me."

Any temptation Conway might have

had to try and bluff Talbot was killed off by the knowledge that Walt Martin had been with him when they found the dead man, but he could not let this opportunity slip by without giving Talbot a warning.

"The next time any man tries to kill either me or Sheriff Gilpin, I'll arrest you as an accessory before the fact, and don't you forget it."

* * *

Conway was careful not to glance in the direction of Joe Blondell as he descended the stairs and crossed the bar room. He knew the gambler needed little provocation to reach for his guns.

The two men knew each other well after the time they had spent together in Yuma more than four years earlier, then setting themselves against each other in a battle of wits in the chase for that stolen government money. Blondell had been right, he could have killed Conway several times over and would have done had it not served his purpose to let him live. Now he was a man with hate in his heart, built up over the years he had been trailing the federal agent who had cheated him out of the best nest-egg he was ever likely to get his hands on.

Outside on the boardwalk Conway let out a sigh of relief that Blondell had stayed in his chair. As long as the gambler remained in Buzzards Creek he would be a constant threat.

* * *

Roger Talbot descended the stairs slowly only moments after Conway left his office, the deputy's warning already dismissed from his mind. When he saw Joe Blondell sitting alone he ambled across to his table and sat opposite him.

Blondell raised his eyes to meet those of the tycoon. "You want something from me, Talbot?"

"Our new deputy sheriff tried to give

me the impression last night that you and he were old friends, only I've decided whatever is between you is not friendship."

"No, it ain't. So what?"

"I don't like Conway any more than you do. I'd like to see him gone from Buzzards Creek, only I figure the only way that is likely to happen for a while is if he ends up in a pine box."

Blondell chewed on the implications of what Talbot had said for barely a minute, then more out of curiosity than serious intent he asked, "How much are you offering, Talbot?"

"Five hundred on the day they bury him."

Blondell's laugh was full of contempt. "Come back when you're ready to double it."

14

THE sun was still bright as Conway emerged from the Gold Dust House and he pulled his hat an inch lower to shield his eyes. As he turned right and then right again off Main Street he saw Doc Rickman step up to the door of the Sheriff's Office. A half minute later Conway followed him through the door.

The medic was already seated, an expression of gravity on his face as he turned to see who had come in behind him.

"Deputy."

"Hi, Doc. You look a mite worried."

Rickman looked back at the sheriff. "We've got trouble. Big trouble."

Conway eased his butt onto the edge of the desk and faced the medic.

"What kind o' trouble, Doc?" Gilpin queried.

"Syphilis."

"Syphilis! You mean that . . . "

"One of the most contagious diseases known to man. You'll have to close down the Gold Dust."

Gilpin's eyes slowly lifted to meet Conway's gaze. It was the breakthrough he had prayed for, yet the gravity of Doc Rickman's pronouncement prevented him from smiling with delight. He looked back at the doc.

"You sure about this?"

"Absolutely. I've just examined one of Talbot's women. She has all the second stage symptoms."

Conway snapped. "Second stage?"

"That's right." The doc's gaze flitted from one to the other. "Body rash, headaches, sore throat, mouth and genitalia sores, pain when passing water. The problem is, how many men has she passed it on to?"

"Hell!" the sheriff barked. "Which one is it?"

"Phoebe."

"Oh, no. She's the most popular

woman Talbot ever had in that place. He's used her himself."

"But not recently. I asked her."

"Pity," Gilpin said with disappointment. "If she's passed it on to any man I could have wished it was him."

"Your prejudices are showing, Sheriff," Doc Rickman said.

Conway stood up and looked down at the doc. "No known cure, is there, Doc?"

"They're working on it back east, but there's nothing I can do for the woman. I've advised her to take the next train out of here and head for New York City. It's her only chance, but unless they've come up with a miracle cure I don't know about, there's not much hope for her."

The sheriff asked, "You get a list of names of the men she's been with, Doc?"

"As many as she could remember. She asked me not to tell them until after she's left town. She said she'd take the night train at seven."

"Did you make her any promises?" Gilpin queried.

"A few more hours won't make any difference to the men. I'll ask them all to come in and see me as soon as they can."

Gilpin's comment held bitterness. "Much good that'll do 'em."

"At least I'll know which of them to warn after I've asked the right questions."

The doc sighed. "You want I should come with you to tell Talbot?"

"That would be helpful, Doc. Then he can't accuse me o' shuttin' him down without evidence."

"All right, but let's leave it until around eight o'clock, shall we? You don't want the murder of that woman on your hands, do you? Besides, I'd like my supper to settle first."

"We'll see you in the saloon around eight then. Conway, one of us had better see who gets on that train at seven. You'll be eatin' around that time, so I guess it'd best be me."

* * *

Activities were just beginning to warm up when the two lawmen entered the Gold Dust House. They noticed Roger Talbot in earnest conversation with one of his whores at the foot of the stairs. There was no sign of Doc Rickman, but he came in only two minutes later, just as Talbot saw them and glared his lack of pleasure.

"Let's get this over with, Sheriff," Rickman said, heading in Talbot's direction.

"A quiet word in your office, Mr Mayor, if you please." The doctor's tone intimated that it was more than a request.

"What's the problem, Doc?"

"I think you'd better hear it in private, unless you want these men" — he gazed around him — "to lynch you."

Talbot's face clouded and his mouth tightened. He seemed about to protest at such a suggestion, but he knew

Rickman was not a man with a raw sense of humour. He turned and headed for the stairs, the three men following him, watched by the curious stares of some of the men and women sipping their drinks.

Turning to face his visitors as Conway closed the office door behind him, his face grim, Talbot snapped, "Just what did you mean by that remark downstairs, Doc?"

"Your women are spreading venereal disease amongst the men who frequent this place. Citizens as well as drifters."

"I don't believe it." His tone belied his words. The sudden decision of Phoebe to head for New York City to get the help of a specialist for her problems now made more sense, but he was reluctant to accept the implications. "Prove it."

The sheriff barked, "He don't have to prove it, Talbot. All I have t'do to get you lynched by the mob is announce loud an' clear why I'm closin' you down."

"You can't do that!"

"I can an' I will. Spreading a contagious disease is a federal offence." Gilpin was not sure if that was true or not, but he guessed Talbot wouldn't know, either. "Now we can do this the hard way or you can make it easy on yourself, take your choice."

Talbot's eyes searched first one face and then the others. There was murder in his eyes but none of his visitors flinched under the silent threat.

"Onc o' these days, Gilpin, I'll put a bullet in you."

"You ain't man enough t'do that."

Lips curling contemptuously, Talbot sneered, "Just because I don't go around with a gun sitting on my thigh like you doesn't mean I don't know how to use one."

The doc said, "We're not here to talk about guns, Talbot. Now let's get back to the problem."

Talbot's eyes lost none of their venom as he faced Doc Rickman, but before he could make any further comment the sheriff gave his instructions.

"Now here's what you do, Talbot, if you wanna make it easy on yourself. You go down and close the bar, herd your women up to their rooms, an' then you tell the men you're closing early. You can make whatever excuses you like, but do it! Now!"

For almost a half minute it looked as if Talbot was not going to obey the command, until Conway spoke up, a questioning lilt in his voice.

"Maybe you'd prefer me and the sheriff to do it for you?"

The suggestion galvanized Talbot. "No, I would not!" he snarled as he pushed past them to the door, then turned and added. "You three are dead. Not one of you will be in church on Sunday!"

He closed the door behind him, but the sheriff led the way out on to the landing. The three men stood listening, trying to catch Talbot's words as he issued his instructions. It seemed he was being discreet about it and they failed to distinguish what was said until the clientele began their protests. Then Talbot's good-humoured responses reached them.

"It's only for tonight, fellers. We'll be open again tomorrow, never fear."

The gamblers voiced their objections in support of the drinkers, but Talbot showed remarkable patience with them.

"Come back tomorrow fellers. Everything will be the same tomorrow. Give you a chance to try the beer down at Murphy's place tonight."

As the women came up the stairs in ones and twos the sheriff remarked with a grin, "I'll gamble it hurt him to say that."

When the protests continued the sheriff led the other two down the stairway, ready to help usher the men outside if it should prove necessary. Conway was glad to see that Joe Blondell was nowhere around. Maybe he had gotten himself a game down at the Stag's Head Saloon.

When the last customer disappeared

through the door Talbot turned and saw Doc Rickman, Conway and the sheriff standing at the foot of the stairs. "Now you! Out! All three of you."

The trio moved forward, led by Gilpin. "Just one thing, Talbot. You don't open those doors again until you get my sayso, understand?"

"Go to hell!"

"I reckon you're more likely to end up there."

As they stood on the boardwalk outside the questions leapt from one man to another amongst the ousted clients, some of whom were already heading towards the Stag's Head, while others had moved only a few yards. They spotted the sheriff, Doc Rickman and Conway and one of them came forward to ask, "What's goin' on, Sheriff? Did you make Talbot close up early?"

"That's right. Can't say much about it right now, boys, in case there's a court case in the near future."

"Court case?"

"That's all I'm sayin' right now, so why don't you go down an' sample the beer at Murphy's, like Talbot suggested. Whiskey tastes the same in the Stag's Head as it does any place else."

"Somethin' mighty funny goin' on if you ask me," one man voiced suspiciously.

As the men sauntered down the street Doc Rickman snorted, "Dammit! We should've told Talbot to get his women out of town before the news gets out about Phoebe."

"You think he would have taken any notice?" Conway asked.

"He'd better," the sheriff said. "We don't want them offerin' their services on the street. I'll go round the back an' tell him to make sure they're all on the mornin' train tomorrow."

"And if they're not?"

"We'll have to arrest them and throw 'em in jail 'til they see sense, Conway."

15

THE women were huddled together on the landing when Talbot climbed the stairs again.

"What's going on, boss?" Glenda Garfield asked.

Talbot glared at the four of them. "How many of you knew that Phoebe was poxed up to the eyeballs?"

"We didn't. She told me she'd been to see Doc Rickman this morning," Glenda admitted, "and he'd told her to go to New York for treatment. That's when she told me."

"And what about the rest of you? How many of you have got a body rash?"

Feeling affronted by the suggestion, their denials were heated.

"I'm clean!" Glenda snapped. "You want to come into my room and have me strip off to prove it?"

"I'll take your word for it, Glenda. The rest of you willing to have Doc Rickman examine you?"

"Sure, why not?" they answered one after the other.

Alerted by the noise of conversation downstairs, Talbot turned and went down again, to find Sheriff Gilpin asking the barkeep where he, Talbot, was.

"I'm here, Gilpin. Now you go and get that damned doctor and tell him to get in here pronto. I want my girls examined and given a clean bill of health."

"My advice to you is t'get 'em out o' town on the mornin' train, Talbot. Whether they're healthy or not, when word gets around why Phoebe left in such a hurry the men in this town'll be lookin' for blood, an' most of it'll be yours."

Overhearing what the sheriff was saying, Glenda Garfield hurried down the stairs. "Are you suggesting the men will attack us girls?"

"That's just what I'm suggestin', Glenda. Take my advice an' be on that train in the mornin', an' tell the others I said so."

"To hell with your advice, Gilpin!" Talbot snarled. "Get that sawbones in here. I want these women given a clean bill of health."

"Ain't nothin' stoppin' them visitin' the doc privately, if they feel the need. Goodnight, Glenda. Remember what I said."

As he turned on his heels to leave the sheriff could feel the hatred oozing out of Talbot. A smile of satisfaction touched his lips. He figured he'd gotten Talbot rattled enough to make that mistake Conway had hinted was needed for them to nail him.

What would it be?

* * *

When the women suggested to Talbot that taking the sheriff's advice might be in their best interests he considered it for no more than thirty seconds.

"If you'd feel safer getting out of town, then you do that. I can soon find replacements for all of you."

He marched into his office and plonked himself down in an easy chair to consider his options. There were other men in town who had no love for Sheriff Gilpin, and one in particular had returned to Buzzards Creek that very day. Virgil Washington had just been released from jail, put there three years ago on evidence gathered by Sheriff Gilpin. It should be easy enough to persuade the outlaw to put a bullet into the lawman.

Then there was Joe Blondell, a man with a grudge against Deputy Conway. Blondell had sneered at the offer of five hundred dollars to get rid of Conway, but would he turn down a thousand? It would be worth it to rid himself of all opposition to his ambitions.

Talbot put on his coat, reached for the broad-brimmed flat-topped hat on the peg, and headed down the stairs for the rear exit.

"I'm going out, Ned," he told the barkeep. "Keep an eye on the place while I'm gone."

"Sure, boss."

The Stag's Head Saloon was crowded with regulars and the men who had been evicted from the Gold Dust House. Talbot stood just inside for a while, his eyes raking faces. When he failed to spot Virgil Washington he edged slowly further in, answering the questions being thrown at him concerning the reason for closing down his own establishment so early in the evening with nothing but a polite nod and an accompanying smile.

He noticed that Joe Blondell had managed to ingratiate himself into one of the poker games, but he did not appear to be faring quite as well as he had the previous night in the Gold Dust House. It brought some satisfaction to Talbot, who assumed that Blondell would be more amenable to his renewed offer if he had a losing night.

Virgil Washington had a sour expression on his face as he stood by the bar with a half empty glass of beer. Talbot weaved his way towards him, only to find himself confronted by Sean Murphy.

"What brings you here, Talbot?"

Talbot smiled disarmingly. "As you will already know, Gilpin has closed me down. Thought I'd come along and see how much good it was doing you. I guess you'd like it this way every night."

"A bit too crowded for my liking. I'm not too keen on some of the riff-raff who usually haunt your place, either."

"Think of the money they're bringing you. You don't mind if I sample your beer? I was making my way to the bar."

Murphy stood aside to let him pass. "I don't think you'll have any cause to complain."

Sidling up alongside the morose looking Virgil Washington, Talbot ordered himself a beer and instructed the apron to give Virgil another one.

"Thanks, Mr Talbot. Mighty civil of you."

"You gotten any plans, Virgil?"

"A few."

Talbot leaned closer and lowered his voice. "Drop in and see me later. I'll leave the back door unlocked. I've gotten a proposition I think will interest you."

Washington brightened visibly. "I'll do that, Mr Talbot."

He drained the half in his old glass and picked up the one Talbot had bought him.

* * *

Conway stood in the farthest corner of the saloon, talking to one of Sean Murphy's girls. He was listening politely but every few seconds his eyes scanned the thronged room, unaware that the girl was more than a little impressed by his clean-cut features and long, powerful body. She had inquired about his wounded arm, wormed out of him that he had been college educated, that his folks were both still alive, and that he was not exactly enjoying being a deputy sheriff. When she asked why he had taken the job he said, "The sheriff told me he needed help after somebody took a shot at him."

"You need to be careful, Stuart. There are some very unsavoury characters hanging around Buzzards Creek. Mostly they spend their time in Talbot's place, but there are several in here tonight."

No sooner had she issued the warning than she found Sean Murphy standing beside her. "Now don't let our deputy sheriff monopolize your time, Amy. Go smile at some of the others. They might be feeling neglected."

The colour spread on her cheeks as she realized her employer had seen how much she had become fascinated with Conway and she excused herself politely.

"It was nice talking to you, Amy," Conway told her innocently.

Sean Murphy could see the interest was a one-sided affair and knew he could not accuse Conway of keeping the girl from her duties. Men liked talking to pretty women and Murphy entreated his girls to share their time amongst the clientele and not become entangled with any one of them.

"I could see Amy was bothering you, Conway."

"Not at all, Sean. She was giving me the excuse I needed to stand here and keep an eye on what's going on."

"Expecting trouble, are you?"

"Never can tell, but I take it Talbot doesn't normally frequent your establishment?"

"No, he doesn't. That feller he was talking to at the bar might warrant your attention. He's just done three years, sent to jail by our sheriff. Virgil Washington, by name, and I don't think he's drinking to Gilpin's health."

Joe Blondell was vacating his chair, a forced smile on his face. Conway could not catch the words he exchanged with the other card players but he knew Blondell well enough to assume that Lady Luck had not been sitting on Joe's shoulder that evening. Joe was no quitter, but astute enough to back off when the odds were against him; a strong believer in prudence as opposed to foolishness.

Blondell made his way to the bar, took three or four minutes to empty the whiskey glass he was served while he exchanged a few words with another man leaning on the mahogany, then headed for the door, apparently intent on an early visit to slumberland. Roger Talbot was close behind him, forcing Conway's think-box into more rapid activity.

"Pardon me, Sean, but it's time I made a move."

He stood outside the saloon, close to the wall and away from any light filtering through the draped windows. Talbot and Blondell were in earnest consultation as they walked down the street. There was no chance of Conway picking up the words they exchanged, but he suspected it boded ill for somebody.

Conway followed at a discreet distance, until he saw the two men part company. Blondell headed for the hotel, while Talbot returned to the Gold Dust House. It needed no stretch of the imagination for Conway to realize that Talbot had been attempting to bribe Blondell into action against either Conway himself or Sheriff Gilpin.

Had he succeeded?

Conway stationed himself across the street from the hotel, waiting, but Blondell did not emerge.

* * *

Sheriff Gilpin had remained out of sight for most of the evening, but now that darkness had fallen he prowled the town stealthily. When he saw Virgil Washington emerge from the Stag's Head Saloon, look around furtively, then head for the rear of the buildings, he followed him. With yet another furtive glance behind to make sure he had not been seen, Washington entered the Gold Dust House by the rear door, not smart enough to know that Sheriff Gilpin was adept at surveillance without being observed himself.

The sheriff waited impatiently, accurately guessing that Roger Talbot was offering Virgil Washington an inducement to kill somebody. Talbot would only attempt to do the killing he had threatened if he failed to get somebody else to do it for him. Just how earnestly the threat had been issued was something Gilpin had pondered all evening. It might have been simply bad-tempered bravado but the sheriff was taking no chances.

A few minutes vigilance was all that was needed. Washington reappeared, slinking off towards the sheriff's own office with obvious intent. He paused outside, noticing the light filtering from beneath the door, until the sheriff called out to him.

"You lookin' for me, Virgil?"

Washington whirled around to face Gilpin, his right hand flying to his holstered gun, lifting it with practised ease. The quiet of night was shattered with exploding gunpowder.

16

GUN-FLAME spurted from guns almost in unison with the explosive sounds and Virgil Washington lurched jerkily from the impact of lead thudding into his midriff. A second shot from Sheriff Gilpin's Colt Peacemaker made sure the outlaw would never get up again when his body hit the street.

For a few brief seconds the sheriff and his victim were engulfed in silence, until men who had heard the shots came to investigate the cause of the disturbance. Gilpin felt the tension of his body released as the sound of footsteps approached but he did not turn around: he moved towards the man lying prone on the ground. In broad daylight he would have been convinced the man was dead, but in the darkness he felt the need to make sure. He knelt down beside Virgil Washington and saw that he was no longer clutching his gun, his fingers lying lifeless beside the smoking weapon.

Gilpin reholstered his own gun. Unhingeing his knees and standing tall again, he turned to face the men quickly assembling into a group eaten up with curiosity, and amongst them he noticed Roger Talbot. He moved towards him, ignoring the cries of "What happened, Sheriff?" . . . "Did he brace you right here outside your office?" . . . "It's Virgil Washington. I allus knew he'd come to a sticky end."

The two men faced each other, Gilpin's eyes hard and steady, Talbot's facial muscles twitching in furious disappointment.

"You're under arrest, Talbot."

Talbot's lips curled in a sneer. "On what charge? Being a witness to murder?"

"No. On a charge of incitement to murder. I watched Virgil go into your place an' I saw him come out. As soon as he heard me call to him he went for his gun. You instructed him t'kill me, so don't bother tryin' t'deny it."

Talbot backed away and slotted himself behind other men. When the sheriff moved forward and the men parted he saw that Talbot had a derringer in his right hand, pointed menacingly. As Gilpin's hand clutched his gun butt, Talbot fired, then turned and ran for the rear door of the Gold Dust House.

* * *

Stuart Conway tensed as he heard the gunfire, then forgetting all about Joe Blondell he raced towards the Sheriff's Office, his mind registering that was roughly the location of the explosions. The fourth shot he heard was like a whimper compared with the first three and he guessed it had been fired from a derringer pistol. He arrived on the scene in time to see Sheriff Gilpin clutching at his chest, surrounded by sympathisers.

Gilpin saw him through the mist that clouded his eyes. "Get him, Conway."

"Who was it?"

Several voices spoke in harmony. "Talbot! He shot the sheriff."

"He's gone back into the Gold Dust!" another man yelled.

Conway fisted his Colt .44 and headed for the rear of the whorehouse.

The door was locked. Probably barred on the inside as well, he concluded in frustration. It would need a battering ram to break it down.

A few of the men had followed him. "We need to break this door down, men. Anybody got any ideas?"

Chetwyn Handley spoke up. "There's some six by six in my yard. Come on, fellers, let's get it."

Strange how a man's attitude can change so quickly, Conway reminded himself, recalling how cautious Handley had been whenever the subject of

Roger Talbot's nefarious activities were discussed.

News that Talbot had shot the sheriff spread fast and by the time the men returned from Handley's lumber yard Conway had noticed Ben Casey, George Taggart, Norman Sykes and Harry Digweed in the growing throng. Amongst the last to appear were the Rev'd Brunton, Sean Murphy and Joe Blondell. Joe's hands were on his gun butts as his eyes met Conway's. Conway approached him as the men returned with the battering ram and began pounding the rear door of the Gold Dust House.

"Talbot shot the sheriff, Joe. Would you do me a favour and keep an eye on the front door, just in case Talbot comes out that way?"

Blondell laughed ironically. "He offered me a thousand dollars to kill you, Conway, an' now you want me to kill *him* if he tries to make a break for it?"

"That's life, Joe. You'll never collect

your money now, so you may as well stay on the side of the law. You know very well if you kill a federal officer you'll be on the run for the rest of your days."

"You've got a lotta gall, Conway."

A shout of triumph went up as the door caved in and Conway turned to go back to the task in hand. "Stand back! All of you!"

They cleared the way and Conway stood at the open doorway, listening for the sounds of movement inside, but there was too much of a hub-bub behind him to hear anything. Swiftly he moved inside and hugged the wall, eyes raking the bar room, now in shadow with only the lights from upstairs casting a subdued glow below. Slowly he edged towards the bar, gun in hand, and made sure there was no one hiding behind the mahogany. All he could see was the glint of empty, clean glasses on the shelves under the bar and bottles of beer on those opposite.

Whispered voices, the words too soft for Conway to decipher, came to him from the floor above. Women's voices, he surmised. He stayed listening for a minute or more, wondering where Talbot was and what he planned to do. If he thought he had killed the sheriff he would be feeling more confident about his own position in Buzzards Creek, assuming of course that Joe Blondell had not told him Conway was a federal deputy marshal. On the other hand he might fear the backlash from the townsfolk he must surely know were most supportive of Sheriff Gilpin, plus the fact that it could only be a matter of time before they learned the reason for the Gold Dust House being closed down.

Roger Talbot, Conway decided, was a man in fear, and like a wounded cougar, now at his most dangerous. He would kill if he had to in order to save himself.

Conway cat-footed to the foot of the stairs and peered upwards.

"Drop the gun, Conway. I've got you covered."

Quickly stepping back into shadow, Conway knew a moment later that Talbot had been bluffing. The two shots that he fired hit the foot of the wall opposite the stairway and would have missed their target by at least two feet. Wherever Talbot was situated he had only seen Conway's shadow, not the man himself.

How does he know it's me? Conway asked himself, but a moment later he realized he was the obvious one to go looking for Talbot after the shooting of the sheriff.

"Come on down with your hands in the air, Talbot. You're trapped. There's no way you can escape arrest now."

"If you want me, come and get me!"

Round one to Talbot. Conway would be like a sitting duck target if he attempted to climb those stairs. He thought fast.

"Send your women down, Talbot. We don't want any of them hit by a stray bullet."

"The women stay here!"

Talbot was gambling that Conway would be reluctant to shoot if the women were anywhere near him, which gave him a double advantage. Conway decided to try and provoke him.

"Never figured you as the kind of man to hide behind a woman's skirt, Talbot. Thought you were a man, not a mouse."

"I'm on to you, Conway. You don't get me going with insults."

"Be hard to insult a man who shelters behind petticoats."

"What are you sheltering behind, Conway? You scared to come and get me?"

Not scared, but not stupid, either, Conway told himself.

"I can wait, Talbot. Like I told you, you're trapped."

"I've gotten food and drink and all the time there is. Your patience will crumble before mine."

Talbot had a point, Conway was forced to concede. He considered his options and they seemed very limited. There was a stairway at the side of the saloon leading to the upper floor, a safety feature in case anyone upstairs was trapped in the event of a fire during the night, but Conway figured that would be locked on the inside. Now if only he could create a diversion . . .

"Send those women down, Talbot. They'll be safer down here, out of the line of fire, if you intend this to be a shoot-out."

"That's up to you, Conway. Come on up without your gun and the women will come to no harm."

And I'll be lying dead on the stairs, Conway knew without a doubt. It was stalemate. Conway would have to think more about that diversion. He cat-footed back to the rear door.

"What's going on, Mr Conway?" the Rev'd Brunton asked him.

"He's upstairs, Reverend, and there's no way I can get up there without giving him the chance to blow my head off."

"Let me talk to him. He might listen to me."

A short, derisive laugh pushed out of Conway's throat. "You mean because you were at school together? Forget it, Mr Brunton. He knows his only chance is to kill me, assuming he thinks he's already killed Sheriff Gilpin. How is the sheriff, by the way?"

"Nasty chest wound, I believe. Doc Rickman is tending him."

"How serious?"

"Reckon he'll live, Conway." The verdict came from Ben Casey.

"Good. What we need is a diversion of some sort to get Talbot wondering what's going on. Something to give me a chance to get up those stairs without getting my head shot off."

"You'd stand a better chance if you make him come down to you, Deputy," Chet Handley suggested.

"And how do you suggest we do that, Chet?"

"Burn him out. Get the fire wagon and the men down here in case we need 'em to stop the fire spreading to other buildings, then set fire to the place."

"There are women up there with him, Chet! We can't risk them being fried alive!"

"They won't be. There's a stairway round at the side for them to get down. We'll start the fire this end."

You mean do what you've always feared he would do to you if you didn't keep paying him that ten percent, Conway figured, but he didn't voice the thought. He could see Chetwyn Handley was relishing the prospect of seeing the Gold Dust House go up in smoke. He didn't care if Roger Talbot fried or made his escape with his women. If he elected to come down out of the inferno he could be arrested for the attempted murder of Sheriff Gilpin, and that would curtail his activities for some considerable time. And Handley was not the only one who would benefit from that fact.

"I'm a peace officer, Chet. I can't get involved in arson. You'll have to come up with a better idea than that."

The Rev'd Brunton offered to help. "Let me go in there and engage Talbot's attention while you creep up those stairs and see if you can get inside that way?"

"It's hardly likely, Reverend. Talbot will have thought of that himself."

"But the women will want to get out if they fear there's any danger to themselves."

"That's true. All right, let's give it a try, but don't trust him enough to let him put a bullet in you."

Brunton went inside, while other men crowded the doorway. As he stood for a few moments allowing his eyes to grow accustomed to the gloom, he felt the reassuring hardness of the gun he was carrying in an inside pocket of his long coat.

Stepping cautiously towards the foot of the stairs, he palmed the revolver and held it in readiness for action, should the need arise. Then he called out, "Roger! It's Dave Brunton. Why don't you give yourself up and save everybody a lot of grief?"

Talbot came to the head of the stairs, confident he was safe from the man he had bullied as a boy. "Stay out of this, Dave. Stick to your preaching. This is my fight and I intend to win it. You tell that to Conway. He can't hide behind you."

"I don't think he's that kind of man, Roger. Surrender now and it will go well with you in court, but if you start shooting at people they'll send you down for a long spell."

"Nobody's sending me anywhere, Dave. Once Conway's dead things will get back to normal, now I've gotten rid of Gilpin."

"You're wrong, Roger. You only wounded the sheriff. They can't hang you for that, but they will if you kill anyone else."

"Don't try bluffing me, Dave. I shot him plumb in the chest. I was too close to miss."

Brunton figured Conway needed more time to get up those outside stairs and make an entry, so he needed to hold Talbot's attention for a while longer.

"Some of the men are threatening to burn you out, Dave, so think of the ladies you've gotten up there with you."

If the women had heard him they would be anxious for their own safety, in which case they would almost surely head for the upper exit door, unlocking it for Conway to make his entrance.

"They wouldn't dare!"

"You're wrong, Roger. You've angered too many of them. They remember how you ordered the Osbourne homestead to be torched. It's what they call poetic justice."

The long silence convinced Brunton that he had played his trump card.

Talbot would now be fighting the one threat he feared more than any other. Brunton rubbed salt in the wound.

"This place will burn like matchwood, Roger. A spell in jail is better than being burnt alive."

17

CONWAY stood on the landing outside the private exit door for a couple of heartbeats, listening for sounds of movement inside. Colt pistol in his right hand, he used his left to turn the handle on the door and gently pushed. It remained firmly shut. He pressed his ear to the woodwork, trying to hear Roger Talbot's responses to whatever the Rev'd Brunton was saying to him from below. The words were faint and indistinct.

The smell of kerosene wafted his way on the breeze. Handley, it seemed, had ignored his warning and was intent on smoking out Talbot, with potentially drastic results.

Conway raced back down the stairway and around to the other end of the building. He was too late. The whoosh of flames climbing the timber walls drove him back. There was no time for protests and he turned and ran back up the outer stairs. As he reached the landing again the door opened and the women stared at him in fright, then rushed past him in headlong flight.

Stepping inside, Conway heard gunshots and rushed towards the inner staircase. Halfway down he spotted Roger Talbot and called out, "Drop the gun, Talbot!"

Talbot whirled round and fired two shots from a Smith and Wesson revolver, making Conway throw himself to the floor, but one bullet creased his ribs as he went down.

Racing back up the stairs, Talbot pointed his gun at Conway with the intention of finishing him off, but before he could squeeze the trigger his body lurched violently and he lost his balance as two bullets from Conway's gun pumped into him.

Talbot overbalanced and fell backwards down the stairway, dead before his body came to rest alongside the inert form of the Rev'd Brunton. Scrambling to his feet, Conway hurtled down the stairs and saw Brunton lying there, the gun with which he had earlier tried to kill Conway two feet away. There was a blood stain on the preacher's chest but his eyes were open and Conway could see he was still alive.

He holstered his gun and got a hold on Brunton under the armpits, felt his own unhealed wound protest in pain as he dragged the tall cleric towards the back door. Smoke was beginning to fill the bar room and Conway coughed as he reached the door.

"Help me get him out!" he yelled at men standing watching the conflagration.

Two of them rushed forward and took charge of Brunton, who groaned in agony as he was roughly handled.

"Get him away from here and tell Doc Rickman to see what he can do for him."

Turning to go back inside to retrieve the body of Roger Talbot, Conway saw at once that it was a forlorn gesture. The flames had already spread across the doorway and the timber building was burning furiously. Anger mounted within him and threatened to make him lose his equilibrium. He silently vowed to punish Chetwyn Handley for his vicious act.

He turned and followed the man who had taken charge of the Rev'd Brunton, thankful to see he was still alive. Roger Talbot had not been much of a marksman. Three times he had attempted to kill in the last twenty minutes, but the sheriff, Brunton, and Conway himself had all survived, albeit each of them wounded.

* * *

Conway watched the flames completely consume the Gold Dust House, his left hand clutching his wounded side. The wound in his arm had been reopened and blood trickled down to join that already staining his hand. Just a few yards away to his right the whores gazed in dismay as every stitch they owned, apart from what they stood up in, was consumed by the flames. At least they'd had the sense, Conway correctly surmised, to grab any money they had on the premises. And Talbot would know nothing about it as the fire charred his lifeless body, a fact which gave Conway some comfort. The man had brought upon himself his own demise.

An hour later, his own wounds dressed by Doc Rickman, Conway stood looking down at the sheriff. Gilpin looked back at him.

"What happened, Conway?"

Conway told him, making a point of explaining how the Rev'd Brunton had played his part in bringing the reign of Roger Talbot to an ignominious end, risking his own life in the process.

"Will he make it?"

"Doc says he has a fifty-fifty chance. The bullet was buried in his chest, only an inch from his heart. Doc Rickman had to dig deep to get it out. The operation caused more damage, but we're hopeful."

"That man ain't like no preacher I ever knew."

Conway smiled. "I don't think he'll be buying another gun now that Talbot is dead. He's lost the one he had in the fire."

The sheriff's eyes shuttered and his head slowly tilted sideways. Conway left him to sleep and headed for his own bed. Wearied almost beyond rational thought, as he undressed he felt little satisfaction from knowing that his purpose in coming to Buzzards Creek had been accomplished.

* * *

Valerie Underwood did not disturb him. She had heard all about how he had saved the life of the preacher and been wounded himself in the trouble that had brought an end to strife in the town, and knew he needed the extra rest. The sun was approaching its zenith by the time he put in an appearance.

Shame-faced, he looked at the little woman. "I guess I must have been tired last night."

"It was late when you got to bed. I thought I'd best let you sleep. You ready to eat?"

"I am a mite peckish," he admitted, almost apologetically.

* * *

Sheriff Gilpin was awake but looking wan. "Hi, there, Conway. You're not lookin' so good yourself."

"Talbot creased my ribs last night. Doc says a couple of them are cracked. He reckons I'll have pain for about three weeks before it begins to ease off. Tells me I have to take it easy."

"You mean I need a new deputy in a hurry?"

"I reckon."

"Any suggestions?"

Conway grinned. "How about Joe Blondell?"

"Blondell!" Gilpin was astounded by the suggestion, but Conway gave him a couple of minutes to get used to the idea. "You think he'd take the job?"

"I have my doubts, but from what I've seen of the citizens around Buzzards Creek, I'd say he's the best man for the job."

"Go get him then, but don't tell him why I want to see him. I want to see his face when we put the idea to him. Should be the best tonic a wounded man could have."

* * *

Blondell stared from one to the other, amazement registered all over his face.

"You two have more gall than that Talbot." He looked at Conway. "Would have served you right if I'd taken that thousand dollars he offered me, Conway."

"I understand how you feel, Joe, but

neither me nor the sheriff are fit enough to keep order around here right now. It occurred to me you might find the challenge a nice change from losing money in the Stag's Head Saloon."

"Don't pay much," Gilpin put in, "but you come highly recommended, Blondell."

As Blondell switched his gaze back and forth from the man lying in his bed and the handsome deputy federal marshal, he came to the conclusion that Conway must hold him in high regard. That fact at least went some way to appeasing his grievance at the loss of five thousand dollars four years earlier.

"Well . . . I guess the townsfolk don't want Buzzards Creek slippin' into lawlessness."

Conway unpinned the star on his vest and handed it across to Blondell. "Your first job, Joe, will be to arrest Chetwyn Handley on a charge of arson."

Blondell shook his head. "Sorry, Conway, but I can't do that. You see, it might have been Chet who put forward the idea, but it was the other men who latched on to it. Handley just stood around grinning as the kerosene was brought and splashed all over the walls, then set alight. We'd never get a charge of arson to stick in court."

A surge of satisfaction coursed through Conway. The thought of Chet Handley being charged had not brought him much joy.

"In that case, Joe, I'll leave you to it. Time I paid the preacher a visit."

He paused with the bedroom door half open as the sheriff asked Blondell, "What happened to Talbot's women?"

"They did some shoppin', got the banker to open up early so's they could withdraw their savin's, then caught the mornin' train by the skin o' their teeth. Lucky for them it was a half hour late gettin' in. The townswomen all have smiles on their faces."

There was a smile on Conway's face as he closed the door softly behind him.

Other titles in the Linford Western Library:

TOP HAND
Wade Everett

The Broken T was big. But no ranch is big enough to let a man hide from himself.

GUN WOLVES OF LOBO BASIN
Lee Floren

The Feud was a blood debt. When Smoke Talbot found the outlaws who gunned down his folks he aimed to nail their hide to the barn door.

SHOTGUN SHARKEY
Marshall Grover

The westbound coach carrying the indomitable Larry and Stretch headed for a shooting showdown.

FIGHTING RAMROD
Charles N. Heckelmann

Most men would have cut their losses, but Frazer counted the bullets in his guns and said he'd soak the range in blood before he'd give up another inch of what was his.

LONE GUN
Eric Allen

Smoke Blackbird had been away too long. The Lequires had seized the Blackbird farm, forcing the Indians and settlers off, and no one seemed willing to fight! He had to fight alone.

THE THIRD RIDER
Barry Cord

Mel Rawlins wasn't going to let anything stand in his way. His father was murdered, his two brothers gone. Now Mel rode for vengeance.

ARIZONA DRIFTERS
W. C. Tuttle

When drifting Dutton and Lonnie Steelman decide to become partners they find that they have a common enemy in the formidable Thurston brothers.

TOMBSTONE
Matt Braun

Wells Fargo paid Luke Starbuck to outgun the silver-thieving stagecoach gang at Tombstone. Before long Luke can see the only thing bearing fruit in this eldorado will be the gallows tree.

HIGH BORDER RIDERS
Lee Floren

Buckshot McKee and Tortilla Joe cut the trail of a border tough who was running Mexican beef into Texas. They stopped the smuggler in his tracks.

BRETT RANDALL, GAMBLER
E. B. Mann

Larry Day had the choice of running away from the law or of assuming a dead man's place. No matter what he decided he was bound to end up dead.

THE GUNSHARP
William R. Cox

The Eggerleys weren't very smart. They trained their sights on Will Carney and Arizona's biggest blood bath began.

THE DEPUTY OF SAN RIANO
Lawrence A. Keating and Al. P. Nelson

When a man fell dead from his horse, Ed Grant was spotted riding away from the scene. The deputy sheriff rode out after him and came up against everything from gunfire to dynamite.

FARGO: MASSACRE RIVER
John Benteen

The ambushers up ahead had now blocked the road. Fargo's convoy was a jumble, a perfect target for the insurgents' weapons!

SUNDANCE: DEATH IN THE LAVA
John Benteen

The Modoc's captured thc wagon train and its cargo of gold. But now the halfbreed they called Sundance was going after it . . .

HARSH RECKONING
Phil Ketchum

Five years of keeping himself alive in a brutal prison had made Brand tough and careless about who he gunned down . . .

FARGO: PANAMA GOLD
John Benteen

With foreign money behind him, Buckner was going to destroy the Panama Canal before it could be completed. Fargo's job was to stop Buckner.

FARGO: THE SHARPSHOOTERS
John Benteen

The Canfield clan, thirty strong were raising hell in Texas. Fargo was tough enough to hold his own against the whole clan.

PISTOL LAW
Paul Evan Lehman

Lance Jones came back to Mustang for just one thing — revenge! Revenge on the people who had him thrown in jail.

HELL RIDERS
Steve Mensing

Wade Walker's kid brother, Duane, was locked up in the Silver City jail facing a rope at dawn. Wade was a ruthless outlaw, but he was smart, and he had vowed to have his brother out of jail before morning!

DESERT OF THE DAMNED
Nelson Nye

The law was after him for the murder of a marshal — a murder he didn't commit. Breen was after him for revenge — and Breen wouldn't stop at anything . . . blackmail, a frameup . . . or murder.

DAY OF THE COMANCHEROS
Steven C. Lawrence

Their very name struck terror into men's hearts — the Comancheros, a savage army of cutthroats who swept across Texas, leaving behind a bloodstained trail of robbery and murder.

SUNDANCE: SILENT ENEMY
John Benteen

A lone crazed Cheyenne was on a personal war path. They needed to pit one man against one crazed Indian. That man was Sundance.

LASSITER
Jack Slade

Lassiter wasn't the kind of man to listen to reason. Cross him once and he'll hold a grudge for years to come — if he let you live that long.

LAST STAGE TO GOMORRAH
Barry Cord

Jeff Carter, tough ex-riverboat gambler, now had himself a horse ranch that kept him free from gunfights and card games. Until Sturvesant of Wells Fargo showed up.

McALLISTER ON THE COMANCHE CROSSING

Matt Chisholm

The Comanche, McAllister owes them a life — and the trail is soaked with the blood of the men who had tried to outrun them before.

QUICK-TRIGGER COUNTRY

Clem Colt

Turkey Red hooked up with Curly Bill Graham's outlaw crew. But wholesale murder was out of Turk's line, so when range war flared he bucked the whole border gang alone . . .

CAMPAIGNING

Jim Miller

Ambushed on the Santa Fe trail, Sean Callahan is saved by two Indian strangers. But there'll be more lead and arrows flying before the band join Kit Carson against the Comanches.

GUNSLINGER'S RANGE
Jackson Cole

Three escaped convicts are out for revenge. They won't rest until they put a bullet through the head of the dirty snake who locked them behind bars.

RUSTLER'S TRAIL
Lee Floren

Jim Carlin knew he would have to stand up and fight because he had staked his claim right in the middle of Big Ike Outland's best grass.

THE TRUTH ABOUT SNAKE RIDGE
Marshall Grover

The troubleshooters came to San Cristobal to help the needy. For Larry and Stretch the turmoil began with a brawl and then an ambush.

WOLF DOG RANGE
Lee Floren

Will Ardery would stop at nothing, unless something stopped him first — like a bullet from Pete Manly's gun.

DEVIL'S DINERO
Marshall Grover

Plagued by remorse, a rich old reprobate hired the Texas Trouble-shooters to deliver a fortune in greenbacks to each of his victims.

GUNS OF FURY
Ernest Haycox

Dane Starr, alias Dan Smith, wanted to close the door on his past and hang up his guns, but people wouldn't let him.

DONOVAN
Elmer Kelton

Donovan was supposed to be dead. Uncle Joe Vickers had fired off both barrels of a shotgun into the vicious outlaw's face as he was escaping from jail. Now Uncle Joe had been shot — in just the same way.

CODE OF THE GUN
Gordon D. Shirreffs

MacLean came riding home, with saddle tramp written all over him, but sewn in his shirt-lining was an Arizona Ranger's star.

GAMBLER'S GUN LUCK
Brett Austen

Gamblers seldom live long. Parker was a hell of a gambler. It was his life — or his death . . .